POSSESSED

POSSESSED

A Lost Novel of the Occult

ROSALIE AND EDWARD SYNTON

With an introduction by
JOHNNY MAINS

This edition first published in 2025 by
The British Library
96 Euston Road
London NW1 2DB
bl.uk

1 3 5 7 9 10 8 6 4 2

Possessed was first published in 1927 by Hutchinson and Co., London.
Introduction © 2025 Johnny Mains
Volume copyright © 2025 The British Library Board

Represented in the EU by Authorised Rep Compliance Ltd., Ground Floor,
71 Lower Baggot Street, Dublin, D02 P593, Ireland. arccompliance.com

Cataloguing in Publication Data
A catalogue record for this publication is available from the British Library

ISBN 978 0 7123 5539 1
e-ISBN 978 0 7123 6225 2

Cover and frontispiece design by Mauricio Villamayor
with illustration by Mag Ruhig
Text design and typesetting by Tetragon, London
Printed in England by CPI Group (UK) Ltd, Croydon, CR0 4YY

MIX
Paper | Supporting
responsible forestry
FSC
www.fsc.org   FSC® C013604

CONTENTS

Rosalie and Edward Corse-Scott. Rosalie's photograph is dated
December 1937, perhaps from her entry into New Zealand. Edward's
may be from the same time. Photographs courtesy of the authors'
grandson, John, from Margaret Corse-Scott's collection.

INTRODUCTION

This essay aims to serve as the most comprehensive account
of the lives of Rosalie and Edward Corse-Scott.[1] As they are
completely unknown to genre researchers and readers, I have
deliberately included as many verifiable details as possible, even
those that might seem tangential, to establish a foundational
text for any future research. Please understand that I have sadly
been unable to find out as much about Rosalie; unfortunately,
this is often the case with women whose documentary
history has been overshadowed by their husbands'. As a
result, this essay rests heavily on the life and work of Edward,
for which there are more accessible sources to hand.

JM

After the annihilation of around 886,000 British soldiers during
the Great War, the 1920s witnessed the interrelation of psychiatry,
occultism and literature, with each discipline seeking to interpret
the unseen forces and profound sorrow that defined Britain's post-
war existence. Psychoanalysis analysed survivors and citizens, occult
rituals sought to bring back the whispers of the island's dead, and
literature dramatised the turbulence of the aftermath. This slowly
allowed society to grapple with trauma, identity and modernity.
From these interweaving approaches came brilliant works of fiction.

---

1 Records from the couple's life render their surname with and without the hyphen;
Edward published books as "Corse Scott", but the hyphenated version appears in the
majority of the legal documents.

One of those, a well-reviewed and popular novel of its day called *Possessed* (1927), by Rosalie and Edward Synton (real name Corse-Scott), somehow slipped into the mists of obscurity and remained hidden until I accidentally came across mention of it in a newspaper while hunting lost ghost stories for my British Library anthologies. The more research I did on it, the more remarkable it seemed that *Possessed* hadn't been discovered and championed by the many genre researchers who had come before me. What's more, it had been published by Hutchinson & Co.,[1] who were no strangers to publishing speculative fiction and spiritualism works in the Twenties; they also published the ghost stories of May Sinclair and E. F. Benson during this period. This discovery of *Possessed* makes me wonder if there are more gems to be found by poring over their catalogue from this era.

Light: A Journal of Psychical, Occult and Mystical Research (July 1927) called *Possessed* "a remarkable story with a rather gruesome plot, dealing with the dangerous side of Spiritualism." The journalist Wilfrid Hugh Chesson (of the famed W. H. Chesson diaries), writing for *The Occult Review* (September 1927), said that *Possessed* was "an occult 'shocker', exciting curiosity in a more weirdly unpleasant mother-in-law than I remember to have hitherto met in my travels through fiction. An atmosphere of fetid hypocrisy portentous of crime accompanies her: she is worthy to be the villainess in a romance by Wilkie Collins."

So, when I finally got my hands on a copy of the book via the British Library's collections, the injustice I felt on its behalf was palpable. It was *really* good and appeared to be an important fictional text published during the spiritualism revival, and it deals with themes such as repression, female power and moral ambiguity while taking

---

1 Hutchinson also published the "colonial edition" of *Dracula* that came out shortly after the Constable edition in 1897.

an inquisitive look at psychiatry/modern science vs supernaturalism. While I'm going to talk briefly about its contents, I personally feel that you've been given too much blurb from the back cover already. I do want you to go in as cold as possible and experience this joyously weird and brooding book. So, if you want a spoiler-free read, stop reading this immediately and go straight to the story, and you can pick it up from here when you're finished.

Dr Toogood is a psychiatrist of Harley Street, whose opening lines tell us that it's been a year since his best friend was hanged for the murder of his mother-in-law. Toogood goes on to say that his friend, John Travers, was caught bang to rights, and so begins the story of John's marriage to Muriel, daughter of Helga Stourcross. One day, Toogood is summoned to Travers' house, where he finds Muriel in a death-like state, and deduces that the mother, Helga, is to blame somehow. Later, he will find out that she's induced John into a similar stupor.

The first part of the book is both clinical, with Toogood seeing John as a medical case more than a character, and emotional, when he realises the "Evil" power that Helga has and deduces that she also has John under her spell. The possibility of the *other* is brought up almost straight away, with Muriel saying this about her mother: "For years—ever since I can remember—she has made a study of the supernatural. I was brought up in an atmosphere of spiritualism, occultism, and all those hateful things. Every Sunday evening we had a séance. When I was only twelve she began to hypnotise me."[1]

The second part of the book is narrated by Travers; it's a more emotional account and really documents Helga's "monstrous"

---

1   Page 61.

influence over Muriel. Again, occultism is mentioned: "And she would tell me of her mother's powers, which she seemed to think omnipotent. How Helga was always interested in the occult; had studied it extensively; had travelled after it; and had found—something. How ever since Muriel could remember she had always possessed this—*power* Muriel called it."[1] It's with desperation that John comes to a terrible conclusion; he must do all he can to save Muriel.

The third and final part of the book is a biographical memoir and is written by Helga's own hand. This documents her descent into the *other*; her discovery that she is *powerful*, the terrible things she does to the people around her. The price she pays really gives this book a darkness that's quite unlike anything else I've read from this time. While Helga's role in *Possessed* echoes the devouring mother figure in Gothic traditions, the novel does things a little differently and centres emotional intelligence and manipulation over logic. This is a reversal of where male characters dominate with reason, and women are irrational. Here, the woman wields emotion as *power* and this, I feel, gives the book remarkable substance and depth. Helga's occult power is personal, internal and emotionally resonant; it also aligns with traditional ideas of female mysticism or second sight.

If this book is the result of Rosalie and Edward's belief in spiritual and psychic phenomenon, and they truly believed in a case like Helga's, of possession by evil spirits, it would make sense that they may have taken a direct interest in that movement. Perhaps they would have attended séances themselves? Edward, at least, was known by *The Occult Review*, who wrote about several of his books.

As to the authorship, what's interesting is the placing of the names; Rosalie's is before Edward's, even though Edward was the

---

1   Page 152.

known, published author. My thoughts are that Rosalie may have taken the lead with the writing of this book (my own feelings are that she co-wrote the second part and wrote all of the last section) and may even have come up with the idea for it. One has to wonder at Rosalie's relationship with her own mother, or indeed how she saw *herself* as a mother. Since she was a kindergarten teacher,[1] one might assume that she was a nurturing and giving person, but who knows! Some deep emotional wells are being tapped into here.

Rosalie and Edward's choice for using Synton as their writing name (and Edward had used Synton before) stems from the first person to be called Corse-Scott. John Corse (born in 1756) was a Scottish surgeon who married Catherine Scott of Sinton (or Synton) in 1800. John changed his surname to Corse Scott (or Corse-Scott) and lived in Ashkirk, over the road from Synton, Selkirkshire. Generations of Corse-Scotts would live there, including Edward's grandfather, Edward William Corse-Scott, who was born and brought up at Sintoncorses, also known as Synton House.[2]

Edward Corse-Scott was born on 3 February 1883, in Buxa, Bhootan, North India, to parents John Corse-Scott and Eugenia Margaret Cameron Money. Edward's sister, Una, was born in 1884 (d. 1915) and their brother Ernle followed in 1886 (d. 1969). Two years after the birth of Ernle, John died in August 1888 at Dharamshala, India, while second in command of 2nd Battalion, 1st Goorkhas. At the time of his death, he had gained the rank of Major. He had been in failing health for some time and was due to be invalided back to the UK. The family immediately moved to England.

---

1 Under "Occupation and Employment" in the 1921 Census, Rosalie's employment is given as "Educationist – Kindergarten".
2 The house was demolished in the 1970s.

Edward enrolled at Wellington College, Crowthorne in 1895 (his brother following in 1899), getting the place as a "Foundationer"—a term given to sons of Army officers who had died in service. Their places were given to them with only nominal fees needing paying. Both brothers left in 1901 (Ernle's early leaving could have been down to a misdemeanour).

Edward was deemed unfit to join the army, dashing his hopes. Every other male relative in his family had made it in, but he was rejected on account of poor eyesight. After leaving Wellington College he took up the profession of a mining engineer, studying in Cornwall and London, then left England in early 1903 to learn on the job in Canada and the United States. He returned to England for a brief spell before setting off to Mexico on the SS *Nicaraguan* on 15 September 1904.[1] While in Mexico he became the chief engineer of a large silver mine called "La Blanca y Anexas" at Pachuca.[2] When the Great War broke out, he joined the 1st Canadian Contingent but couldn't get to Canada due to Mexican rebels cutting railway communications.[3] He made his way to England, via Spain and France. He was with the 90th Winnipeg Rifles in August 1914, then two weeks later joined the Royal Engineers. On 15 January 1915 he was made a temporary Lieutenant and was sent to France,[4] but was severely wounded at Givenchy, where he was shot through both lungs.[5] During that spell in the war he was with the 90th Field Company, and 170th Tunnelling Company, helping with maintaining infrastructure, and

1   Under the "Race or People" section of the passenger list, Edward lists himself as "Scotch". He never saw himself as British, English or Anglo-Indian, and although he never lived in Scotland, he was inheriting what he saw as his bloodline.

2   "To the Editor of the *Ramsey Courier*", *Ramsey Courier*, 15 February 1935.

3   The first expeditionary force to Europe in the First World War.

4   *The Army List*, February 1915.

5   The National Archives holds x-ray scans and medical records dated 1914 pertaining to Edward's chest with "multiple gunshot wounds". Reference: PIN 26/21424.

supporting the movements and operations of the army. He returned to England and met Rosalie Aimée Boyd-Given.

Rosalie was born in the spring of 1889, in Portstewart, Ballyaghran, County Derry. She had a sister who passed away before she was born; Mary Catherine ("Kitty") was born in the first half of 1887, but had died before the end of the year. Rosalie moved to England in 1901. In 1911, aged 21, she was living with her mother Mary Rosa Boyd-Given (c.1855–1926) in Bexhill, Sussex. Mary, now a widow, after the passing of Rosalie's father John Boyd-Given in 1896, was living through "private means" and Rosalie's occupation is not given.

On 23 December 1915, at St Matthew's Church, Bayswater, Edward and Rosalie were married. Looking at the marriage certificate, we see that Rosalie's father had been a Justice of the Peace. He also owned a wine and spirits business ("established 50 years") in Coleraine,[1] the sale of which at his death may have provided Mary the means of looking after herself and Rosalie. At the time of the marriage Edward was living at 14 Cowley Street, Westminster and Rosalie resided at 27 Kensington Gardens Square.

Rosalie and Edward's signatures as they
appear on their marriage certificate.

---

[1] *Belfast News-Letter*, 25 February 1896.

Edward returned to France in 1916, part of the 176th Tunnelling Company, but was injured during the Battle of the Somme,[1] and was invalided out in 1917 as he was deemed "permanently unfit for further service".[2] He was given the Silver War Badge (also known as the Silver Wound Badge).

In 1917 Edward wrote a piece, half reportage, half short story, for the *London Weekly Dispatch* (21 August 1917) entitled "Is War Helping Religion?", which I feel could be an extract from his as yet unpublished memoir, which would appear the following year.

On 20 March 1918, Edward and Rosalie's first child, John, was baptised in St Michael and All Angels parish church, Verwood, and their address on the register is listed as Little Synton, Verwood, Dorset. Little Synton was a large house with considerable acreage and an orchard, no doubt named after Edward's ancestral home in Selkirkshire.[3] A photograph of the house exists, *c.*1929, but I've been unable to trace its exact whereabouts. While the house may have been destroyed during bombing raids in the Second World War, Verwood Museum Trust have confirmed there was a house called Synton which survived the war, and was demolished to make way for bungalows in the 1970s. However, they don't have any evidence connecting it to the Corse-Scotts. Personally, I think that it *is* the house; I find it very difficult to believe that there were two separate houses called Synton and Little Synton, both presumably named after Synton in

---

1 The Somme information has been written by Edward in the margins of *A Notable Record: Some Account of the many families descended in the Male and Female Lines from Daniel Van Renen* by E. Joubert De La Ferte (Hatchards, 1926). Edward and his brother Ernle are listed in this book.

2 From the margins of *A Notable Record*. However, typing Edward's name into the Silver Badge database yields no results. Edward *did* work for the Silver Badge Party in 1919.

3 Apropos of nothing, Verwood churchyard is the burial place of Buster Merryfield, better known as Uncle Albert in *Only Fools and Horses*.

Little Synton, Verwood, Dorset, as seen in an advertisement
for sales enquiries in *Country Life*, 19 October 1929.

the Scottish Borders—although it is possible that the Corse-Scotts
owned and named two houses in the area.

Also in 1918, Edward's quasi-memoir, *Tunnellers All*, was published (written under the Synton name, possibly so as to obscure
his identity). The book contained short tales from the Western
Front, bringing home the realities of the miners' stark underground
warfare with the Germans. Extracts from the book appeared in the
Sheffield Weekly Telegraph from August to October 1918.

In February 1919, *Flight Magazine* ran an article called "Airisms
from the Four Winds", which stated that Edward was looking for
people to join the Silver Badge Party, an anti-Bolshevik league.
Men and women were welcome to join, and it points out that "it's
the great middle class that pays the penalty of inaction against this
treacherous menace."

In July, Edward wrote an article called "The British Miner"
for the *Daily Herald*. In it he talks about his time working with the

miners of America, known as "sandhogs", and Mexico, where the miners are called "barriteros".[1] This is where we see his real socialist colours come through, talking about the horrendous conditions that miners experience, where he openly calls it "the worst trade in existence". He says it's no wonder that British miners would rather work in Patagonia, where conditions are better, and that the average output of a British miner is less than half of a South American's.

The 1921 Census shows the growing Corse-Scott family are living at Bay View, Windsor Mount in Ramsey on the Isle of Man. Rosalie was a private teacher and Edward had turned his hand to farming. On 12 May 1921, *My Three Husbands* was published under the Edward Synton pseudonym, though the book does not feature the author's name on the cover boards or title page. The story shares some themes and ideas with *Possessed*, including spiritualism, and like *Tunnellers All*, features details that may have been drawn from Edward's own experiences in India and in the Great War.

In 1925 Edward summoned David Middlemiss, an ex-servant at his house at Ballagarrow, to court for trespass. David had been stalking the lands with his shotgun, not thinking that his former boss would object. David was subsequently found guilty of wilful trespass and fined 2s. 6d. and costs. It wasn't the only time Edward had been in court; a few months before, he had been summoned to the High Bailiff's court for removing two pigs without a permit. He was fined £1 3s. 4d., and immediately tried to appeal it, saying he was "up against a darned fool law."[2]

In early 1926 Edward put his car up for sale; a Ford Saloon, which was in "excellent condition" and the "price reasonable". This

---

1 "Barreteros" seems to be the accepted spelling today.
2 "Trouble over Pigs", *Ramsey Chronicle*, 13 February 1925.

The Old Vicarage, Padstow, *c.*1927, where
Rosalie and Edward wrote *Possessed*.

was followed by the sale of two small freehold farms, Ballagarrow
and Ballamenagh which he wanted rid of immediately as he was
"declining farming and moving back to the mainland". On 18 March
of this year, Rosalie's mother died. At the start of the year she had
been living at Matlock House on Castle Mona Avenue in Douglas,
on the Isle of Man, but it seems she moved to Hogarth Road,
Earls Court, shortly before her passing. The Corse-Scotts left for
Cornwall, moving to what is now a Grade II listed building, "The
Old Vicarage" in Padstow.[1] It was where Rosalie and Edward wrote
their occult novel *Possessed*,[2] and they even set the exciting parts
of the book in Penzance, just over an hour away. The work was

1 "Splendour of Life", *Cornish Guardian*, 20 November 1930.

2 *Catalog of Copyright Entries* (Library of Congress, 1927). Part 1: Books, Group 1. New
Series, Volume 24, for the year 1927. Entry #8715.

published by Hutchinson on 24 June the following year;[1] however, this event was overshadowed for the authors by the tragic deaths of two of their daughters within two months of each other. They were Rosalie, who was only six, and Una, who was ten. According to probate and birth records, at the time of their passing at least some of the family was living, or staying with somebody, at 57 Warwick Avenue in Bedford. The couple's daughter, Doreen, was also born during this spell in Bedford.

The Daily Herald (6 July 1927) published an absolutely delightful poetical review of *Possessed* by Francis Brown, which is reproduced in full below:

"A PSYCHOLOGICAL MYSTERY"
Possessed, by Rosalie and Edward Synton. Hutchinson, 7s. 6d.

In the Ingoldsby Legends there's plenty of proof
That it's best to beware of the man with a hoof,
For no matter how happy he makes you to-day,
In the end there is always the devil to pay;
And be he Mephistopheles, Nick, or Old Harry,
It's you to the sulphurous region he'll carry!

But the Legends aren't, possibly, nowadays read,
For a lot of folks fancy the Devil is dead.
Yet if you, my dear reader, are one of that lot
You will speedily learn the old reprobate's not,
And your face may—perhaps—take a powdery tint on
When reading this novel by R. and E. Synton.

---

1 *Catalog of Copyright Entries* (Library of Congress, 1927).

For though he now dwells on a psychical plane,
Helga Stourcross did not have to call him in vain,
And the number of people she injured or killed
(For "the Shadow" would do as she wickedly willed)
Makes you guess quite correctly her end will be gory,
And yet there remains a surprise in the story.

The dominant theme of the tale may be this—
And it's one, let me say, that no reader should miss—
But it deals with some perfectly lovable folk,
Though their lives may be any old thing but a joke,
And its telling has merits distinctly exceeding
Most popular fiction now offered for reading.

*

After the book was published it seems that the family moved back to Little Synton, living between Dorset and Cornwall for another two years. By 1930 the couple were back on the Isle of Man, and Edward's next book, *The Splendour of Life*, was published. In his introduction to the book Edward writes: "This book has no special purpose. It was written to lay before responsible men and women certain ideas which the writer, formerly a mining engineer, has linked with life's problems. Many of these ideas came from the great and unchartered ocean of thought and no claim is made that they are new. On the contrary, you will find some that existed before Christianity. It is enough that these thoughts have been written for the seeker after truth by a fellow seeker who was formerly a prospector for gold and silver."

In 1931 their eight-year-old child, Angel, made the pages of the *Ramsey Courier*, when she went missing from a party of blackberry pickers. When she hadn't returned by dusk, a search party of Glen Auldyn residents and two policemen set out to find her. She was found eventually on Mountain Road by the grocer's van driver, Mr Leece, who took her back to her parents.[1]

In 1932, Edward was regaling the members of the Ballaugh Debating Society with his address on "World Chaos and the Way Out", where he was in favour of "scrapping many of the systems at present in use in business, politics, education and government."

In 1934, the family were living in Holly Lodge, Glen Auldyn. In a letter to the Editor of the *Ramsey Courier*, dated 15 February 1935, Edward mentions that Rosalie was against the use of "young men, foodless, workless, doleless and nearly hopeless" if war was ever to rear its ugly head."[2]

In 1935, Edward gave a talk entitled "What Will the Next Civilisation Be Like?", where he talked about the rise and fall of previous civilisations and put forward the needs of the future, saying that "machines of the next civilisation will be the servants, not the masters of man."

In 1936, the *Ramsey Courier* reviewed Edward's two books of poetry, *Something to Say* and *A Psychologist to His Love*, saying that "Mr Corse Scott writes as vigorously as he argues for a certain point of view—not the popular point of view, but more usually the extreme point of view [...] they are worth reading, though everybody will not agree with the sentiments expressed therein."

It finished with a quote from one of his poems, "Who Will Build The New World":

---

1 "Search For Lost Child", 2 October 1931.

2 Edward also says in the letter: "I conceive it to be my duty to-day, as I conceived it my duty in 1914, to fight for peace. To-day that duty is ever more urgent because it is more personal: I happen to be the father of four boys, and they are not going through what I went through if I can help it."

Oh workers, come what will,
You'll build the new world
As you build the old.
See to it then you build
A workers' world,
And not a paradise
For bourgeois parasites.

In late 1936, Edward gave a talk on "The Conquest of Poverty", where his argument was that the troubles of the world were "the self-interest that produced goods for profit and not for use."

From the letters he sent to the *Isle of Man Examiner* (there are many), a picture of Edward emerges as someone who could be described as hard-left, who wanted to smash the system, hated fascists and capitalists and only wanted peace for his fellow man. I really feel that he and I would have got on well.

On 16 December 1937, RMS *Remuera* sailed from Plymouth to London before setting off to Wellington in New Zealand. The passengers included the Corse-Scott family; Edward, Rosalie, John (20), Edward (18), Angel (15), Alexander (13), Margaret (12), Doreen (10) and Michael (8). Their final home, built by themselves, was called "Far Away" at Mangōnui, Northland.

Their expected idyll wasn't necessarily a happy one. "Coming from a middle-class English background and moving to a marginal farm in the middle of nowhere must have been a soul-destroying experience for both the parents and the siblings."[1] Barely eighteen months had passed since their escape from England when Rosalie died on 29 May 1939 at Kaitaia Hospital. She left Edward £369 18s. 2d.

---

1 Email from Rosalie and Edward's grandson, John Herring (Corse-Scott) to Johnny Mains, 2 September 2025.

Edward, Rosalie and their children, from a piece in the *Isle of Man Examiner*,
17 December 1937, captioned "Off to New Zealand". The figure on the right
is explained to be W. H. Chapman, who arranged the Corse-Scotts' passage.

*

For *The Auckland Star* on 17 February 1940, Edward wrote an article
called "A Lasting Peace", which reads:

> There will be a lasting peace only when men love one another
> and would sooner be killed than kill. When fathers have made
> the world fit for children to be born in, and mothers educate
> their children in nobility, world-mindedness and the arts and
> crafts of peace. When little practitioners and national bounda-
> ries have been replaced by the larger patriotism, people are
> proud, not of being the subjects of this or that empire, but

of being citizens of the world. When the captains and the kings have departed, and mankind has taken the next great step up the ladder of progress from "mine to ours" there will be lasting peace. And we can make a start now, in the sure knowledge that this has been the vision of every great poet and the objective of every great mind since men were men. And in the equally sure knowledge that every forward movement of the human race has been and will be started by some individual.

A letter to *The New Zealand Journal of Agriculture* (15 May 1942) sees the last time that Edward's name appears in print during his lifetime. In an article by A. S. Bevin (who was moaning a lot about "stinking fish" and spewing racist tracts against the Japanese) a letter from Edward is quoted, where he says: "People are beginning to realise that the secret of Health—healthy crops, healthy stock, healthy humans—is living soil. Living soil = Humus + Work."

Edward Corse-Scott was driving to his home from Totara North on 31 August 1943, when the steering gear of the car he was driving failed. His car plunged over a ten-foot bank onto rocks on the beach below. His son, twelve-year-old Michael, was miraculously thrown clear and escaped any injury. Probate was granted to Lethbridge Money & Prior, 25 Abingdon Street, Westminster, on 31 October 1944. He left £1,582 10s. 4d. to his son Edward. Probate was sealed on 28 February 1945.

The *Isle of Man Examiner* published an obituary four months after his death and quoted an extract from a letter that Edward had written to the paper, talking about the struggle their family was having in New Zealand: "In this far away home of ours, built with our own hands, and where never a blade of grass grew, we still have dreams of coming back; the children to their birthplace, and myself to the loveliest little land I know. We are now in a country which is a perfect example of Imperialism, the 'spoiling' system that robs the extremities to enrich the centre. Heaven only knows how much treasure has been taken from this land... this was virgin land, fresh from the hand of nature and teeming with riches."

In the letter he went on to say that two of his children had died since coming to New Zealand.[1] A letter to the editor of the same paper, by Edward's friend, Henry A. Rogers, called Edward "a revolutionist", who "had a strong desire to leave the world the better for his influence."[2]

In Plots 73 and 74 in Kaeo Public Cemetery rests a headstone that reads:

IN MEMORY OF

MUM, DAD AND BROTHER ALEC.

ROSALIE AIMEE CORSE-SCOTT

30TH MAY 1939. AGED 50 YEARS.

EDWARD CORSE-SCOTT

31ST AUG. 1943. AGED 60 YEARS.

ALEXANDER CORSE-SCOTT

23RD AUG. 1942. AGED 18 YEARS.[3]

*

It fills me with no end of joy to be writing this introduction. That *Possessed* is now part of the British Library's august Tales of the Weird series and is being reprinted for the first time in a touch under 100

---

1 "Manx Pioneer's Tragic Death", *Isle of Man Examiner*, 31 December 1943.

2 "Exhaustible Resources", 7 January 1944.

3 Alexander was an Air Force Cadet who died in New Zealand. Rosalie's date of death here differs from that of her probate records and may be the date of interment.

years, shows that hidden gems are still out there to be found. I live for finds like this and I really hope you enjoy this weird tome, as I think it is an incredible book, with one of the great female antagonists in Helga Stourcross. I am very proud that it has been brought back to life to possess us all.

JOHNNY MAINS

JOHNNY MAINS is an editor and researcher who specialises in finding "lost" works of genre fiction. Another of his discoveries, *At the Change of the Moon* by Bernard C. Blake, was published by Mislaid Books in 2025.

BIBLIOGRAPHY

By Edward Synton

Tunnellers All (Grant Richards, 1918)
My Three Husbands (Methuen & Co., 1921)[1]
I Want to Be Loved by You (score for a "comedy foxtrot song". Peter Derek, 1932)

By Edward Corse Scott

The Splendour of Life (Rider & Co., 1930)
Something To Say: A Thought Sequence in Modern Form (Self-published, 1935)
A Psychologist to His Love (Self-published, 1935)

By Rosalie and Edward Synton

Possessed (Hutchinson & Co., 1927)

---

1 Curiously, Edward's name does not appear inside the book, nor on the front board and spine. The book is listed as one of his previous publications in the preliminary pages of *Possessed*.

A NOTE FROM THE PUBLISHER

The original novels and stories reprinted in the British Library Tales of the Weird series were written and published in a period ranging across the nineteenth and twentieth centuries. There are many elements of these stories which continue to entertain modern readers; however, in some cases there are also uses of language, instances of stereotyping and some attitudes expressed by narrators or characters which may not be endorsed by the publishing standards of today. We acknowledge therefore that some elements in the stories selected for reprinting may continue to make uncomfortable reading for some of our audience. With this series British Library Publishing aims to offer a new readership a chance to read some of the rare material of the British Library's collections in an affordable paperback format, to enjoy their merits and to look back into the worlds of the past two centuries as portrayed by their writers. It is not possible to separate these stories from the history of their writing and therefore the following novel is presented as it was originally published with minor edits only, made for consistency of style and sense. We welcome feedback from our readers, which can be sent to the following address:

British Library Publishing
The British Library
96 Euston Road
London, NW1 2DB
United Kingdom

POSSESSED

PREFACE
BY DOCTOR TOOGOOD

A year ago my best friend was hanged for murder. The case will be remembered, and caused an unusual stir in legal and medical circles.

There was no reason why he should not have been hanged: he committed murder, on the face of it most foul. No jury of honest men and women could have done otherwise than find him guilty: he pleaded guilty. No judge could have done other than don the black cap: there were no "extenuating circumstances," for the prisoner declined a defence. No Home Secretary, for all our efforts, could conscientiously have mitigated the sentence. Even I, who looked upon him as a brother, realise that as the law is now constituted he was rightly hanged.

And yet John Travers was the best man I have ever known. Right gallantly he went to the gallows, as he would have gone gallantly upon any adventure, however grim. It was by no means the first time he had faced death—"Brother Death," as he used to say.

As a mental specialist of some standing I am used to the unexpected. When Human Nature is hemmed in, hampered, and starved, not only of wholesome food, but of happiness—as is too often the case in these overburdened days—it is apt to become warped and twisted. Abnormalities have almost ceased to surprise the modern psychologist. To us it is rather the normal that is rare: the well-developed, well-balanced brain controlling the well-nourished, well-ordered body.

Of such was John Travers; so normal as to seem in an abnormal world almost abnormal.

If only to refute the garbled reports that appeared in the newspapers, it has always been my intention to give his story to the public. Despite my literary inability, I have looked upon this, to me difficult, task as a duty; not only to his memory; not only to his widow; but to a world which, as yet, judges most superficially, invariably condemns what it cannot understand, and seldom errs on the side of mercy to its fellow-humans.

I, myself, am no whit the better. Relying upon my intimate knowledge of Travers, sundry of his letters that I had retained, and the journal, written in gaol, that he left me, I essayed the task.

For six months the manuscript has lain in my desk. The more I read it, the more I realised to what an extraordinary extent dislike for Helga Stourcross had prejudiced my pen. The woman to me was an unpleasant mystery, and I had made her a monster.

Now this difficulty is overcome. Yesterday evening Muriel, that is, Mrs Travers, brought me what I can only call the most remarkable document I have ever read. It was in her mother's distinctive and almost illegible handwriting, and consisted of sheets torn from a writing-pad, portions of a child's exercise-book, crested notepaper, and when all else had failed, the insides of old envelopes; the whole punctured and tied together with tape.

Certainly an unprepossessing epistle. Muriel explained that it had been sent her by her mother's last landlady, who, carrying out implicit instructions, had retained it for a year.

"If only John had waited," Muriel had said simply. And reading it, I echoed her words. Had John waited but an hour, had this document been in evidence at the time, how different the outcome might have been.

"My mother's soul," Muriel had said. "I never thought she had one. Poor mother!" And so it is christened; so takes its place, untouched, at the end of this volume; which I have not thought fit in any way to alter.

For now the reader can see *around* this singular affair, and should be able to pass a true judgment upon it: as to whether the world gained or lost by hanging John Travers, and as to whether Helga Stourcross was or was not "possessed."

T.P.T.

HARLEY STREET,
LONDON, W.

PART I

Doctor Toogood's Story

I

From boyhood John Travers and I were friends, as his father and my father had been friends before us. Both had been in the same regiment of the Indian Army. Both had been killed in action on the Frontier within a month of each other. And we two fatherless boys had been brought up together. And together gone to Eastchurch College. In age there was only six months between us. But I was always taken to be very much older. For what is age after all but a matter of temperament?

Such was the friendship, too, between Mrs Travers and my mother, that after their widowhood and subsequent return to England, they shared the same house in the Surrey village they had selected for our home. Neither of them married again; not for lack of opportunity, as both were beautiful. Indeed, it seems but yesterday that we boys, like youthful Paris's, were arguing this point. John, always the soul of chivalry, insisting that *mine* was if anything a shade more adorable. And I, not to be outdone, equally determined that *his* should receive the palm.

I question whether there was ever a happier home life than ours. Until the age of thirteen we were educated at home; first by our mothers, who took turns to teach us our first lessons, and later by a tutor, a young Cambridge graduate, who afterwards made his mark in the world of letters as a poet.

With pen in hand it is a sore temptation to dwell upon those delightful days. But our purpose is plain. We must push on, leaving that quiet haven of Love and Peace for the noisy confusion of the modern world.

When Mrs Travers died, of heart failure, John remained with us as a matter of course, my mother being left his sole trustee.

From Eastchurch John passed into Sandhurst, first on the list. How proud we were, my mother and I; in spite of the fact that at the same examination I had only just scraped through, to be subsequently spun on account of defective sight—astigmatism, to be accurate.

John was always a hero to me. Curiously enough he still remains so. The world's verdict alters nothing. For if ever one man *knew* another, from the crown of his head to the innermost recesses of the great heart of him, I knew Travers; the most unselfish and completely manly man it has ever been my good fortune to meet. At school he worked for the school and played for the school; and consequently became head of the school. At Sandhurst he won the Sword of Honour.

In the Army he shone less. Following in the footsteps of a long line of soldiers he was gazetted into the Indian Army. But India was then at peace; and peace-time soldiering, "all child's play and no work," as he put it, did not appeal to him. He was talking of retiring, with a view to he did not know exactly what.

"This is no life for a man," he once wrote to my mother. The letter is before me. "There is nothing I can find here worth working for. It is all a selfish scramble for promotion and pleasure. It is not as you will remember it, not as you and my mother used to picture it by the study fire. The men, inspired by love of country and devotion to duty, holding aloft the torch of English Justice. The women making it easy for their men.

"That was splendid. Now nothing splendid remains. Petty intrigues are the order of the day. Devotion to duty is old-fashioned.

Love of country has become criticism. And English Justice is dying for lack of just men.

"I am seriously thinking of sending in my papers and coming home. It seems to me that the urgent need to-day is for Missionaries of the Right. The world, our world, seems to be growing dark for lack of Love. Men—and women—are needed, it seems to me, to relight the old lamps.

"That would be worth doing."

Whether he would have retired or not is problematic. As it was, the Great War broke out. He was forty then, and held the rank of major.

II

J ohn landed in France with the first Indian Corps. Received the M.C. and a wound in the head that almost proved fatal. And met and married Muriel Stourcross at the latter end of 1915.

Events moved rapidly then.

My dear mother, recently recovered from influenza, contracted a chill at the wedding, at which I officiated as best man, and died some ten days later of septic pneumonia.

The hand of time has healed the wound, but still the scar remains.

She was a good woman, my mother. For one thing I am truly thankful, that she was not alive to see John's ignominious end. It would have broken her heart. As it was, she passed away, one hand in mine and one in John's, so peacefully that we did not know she had gone.

"How beautiful is Death," quoted John when our suspicions were confirmed. And I, heartbroken though I was, could not disagree with him.

III

I t was at John's wedding that I first made the acquaintance of Muriel Stourcross and her mother.

John's wife was one of those women destined to appeal to the mind rather than to the body. Tall, very slim, with fair hair, pale cheeks, and almost bloodless lips, she presented the appearance of a statue in white marble. Her slow, almost stately, movements, soft voice, and lack of colour, enhanced the impression. A statue certainly; living, yet only half alive it seemed. A thing of beauty, not a beautiful woman.

What was the matter with her?

The question rose involuntarily, instantaneously to the mind.

Something was wrong. Undoubtedly she was anæmic, owing to lack of fresh air and fresh food probably. But anæmic would not account for that strange calm, that almost amounted to lack of vitality. Was it merely the effect of acute nervousness? No. If she had nerves, she had them in complete control.

What was the matter with her?

The psychologist in me was vastly interested. Here was something unusual. I found myself examining her, not as John's wife, but as a strange specimen.

Was she the degenerate daughter of a dying race? Many such had come my way to be cured, when there was no cure but death; which is Nature's cure for the incurable. But they, however young, always had the stamp of age about them. However disguised their bodies with Fashion's latest furbelows, however overladen their faces with cosmetics, always they looked at one out of old eyes. And there is about the decadent old age of any species an ugliness that can never be disguised.

Unobtrusively I re-examined my specimen. The great grey eyes were at that moment fixed on John, who was talking to her mother. And I saw that they were love-lit and very beautiful.

No; John's wife was no decadent.

Why, then, that lack of vitality that gave one such an overwhelming impression of the statue, semi-animated?

Vainly I puzzled the question. Then turned my attention to her mother.

IV

Helga Stourcross was a strong woman. I have always looked upon her as one of the most tremendous personalities I have ever come across. Her cleverness was colossal, her emotional capacity enormous, and her determination terrific. The woman was a genius. Had she set herself to constructive, instead of destructive, work, that work must have lived; for the superabundant force that flowed through her must have vitalised it. As it was, the amount of damage she did was almost incredible.

In her young days her appearance is said to have been remarkable. Even at this time, turned sixty as I afterwards discovered, she would have claimed attention in any crowd. Not as so many absurd people attempt to do, by loud behaviour or even louder garments, but by her wonderful figure and superb carriage, which the well-fitting black costume showed off to full advantage. I never knew her wear anything but black.

Her face, too, was remarkable, not for its beauty, of which scarce a trace remained, but for its strength. The eyes dominated the whole. Of a steely blue, the size of the pupils—"drugs" was my immediate thought—made them appear almost black. A lambent fire seemed to lurk behind them, which at times I have seen literally burst out into almost malevolent flame. For the rest, a mouth that was a mere line, chin amazingly strong for a woman, and skin as completely colourless as her daughter's, but crossed and criss-crossed by a thousand lines.

It is a popular superstition that appearances are deceptive. They may seem so to those unversed in the study of appearances. They may be intended to deceive the ignorant, for the purpose of curing ignorance. But to the experienced psychologist appearances are character charts, no more, no less.

My life's business has been the study of men and women, and never have I found two alike. Complexity, outcome of the very vastness of the Creator's mind, is the rule of our world. No two leaves from the same tree, no two peas from the same pod, *nothing*, when examined under the microscope by the expert, is equal. When our little minds, hampered by their own minuteness, go a-building, our new little worlds become nightmares of equality: Equal houses in equal streets, each with its equal square, inhabited by equal people, dressed in equal clothes, eating equal food, doing equal work on equal pay, enjoying equal pleasures, and possessing equal virtues.

In the same way as the manifold and truly marvellous works of Nature to the wise are symbols of God's Mind, so to the intelligent psychologist appearances are essentially the outward and visible signs of inward and spiritual meanings.

From the first I conceived a violent antipathy to Helga Stourcross. Her appearance conveyed to my mind an impression of what I can only call Evil. That lambent fire lurking behind the eyes, that leaden colour, that rat-trap mouth, those multitudinous wrinkles, all depicted Hate. Hate, not fleeting, but enduring. The woman was a genius in embryo. She had heart and head in abundance. Her capacity was enormous. Had her way set fair and had she steered by the stars she must have reached great heights. As it was, for some reason or combination of reasons, she had fallen to great depths.

She stands before me now a picture of magnificent design, but ruined and made hideous by foolish or profane hands—a picture to which I have attached the title of "Tragedy."

V

It quickly became plain to me that my friend Travers had undertaken a far from easy task. For his wife was the only child of this strange woman, who, it was certain, would not lightly loose her hold. It was as "my child" that she spoke of John's wife; and she clearly looked upon her as a personal possession.

How and why she had ever given her consent to the marriage was puzzling. For John was by no means a wealthy man, and, "crocked" as he was, could scarcely have been called a "catch." And it was certain that his wife would never have been permitted to marry without her mother's consent, for anyone less like the modern girl it would have been hard to imagine. Her ill-health, too, would not facilitate matters.

Undoubtedly there were rocks ahead; and the only helmsman who could steer safely past them was Cupid.

Was it a love match?

I looked at them standing there: the man, the statue, and the mother. They were saying good-bye, for it was train time. John's face unusually serious. The statue, sheltering under his shadow, was very still. Helga Stourcross was talking in an intense voice, which one could not fail to hear.

"My poor child! My poor child!" she was pouring out passionately. "This parting will break my heart. I can't bear to lose you. Will you ever think of your poor old mother, I wonder? Ever find time to send her a line—sometimes? Just a word or two on a post card." And so on in a similar strain.

She was the Queen of Tragedy; regardless of all save her own emotions. The stupendous selfishness of her irritated me exceedingly, and I was hard put to it not to interrupt her. Presently she stopped, and I saw that tears were streaming down her cheeks. What an actress the woman would have made!

Meanwhile the statue was smiling softly; a strange smile, half sorrow, half disgust. She certainly was under no delusions about her mother. But from the way she took his arm, the way she clung to him, matching step for step, from the way she looked at him, I knew that she loved John. If John loved her half so well, all would be right. The statue might even come to life. I have known greater miracles.

Amidst a buzz of congratulations they entered the taxi and drove away.

I turned and saw Helga Stourcross staring after them with an expression on her face and a look of cunning malevolence in her eyes not easy to forget. The woman at that moment was positively insane with jealousy. She was dangerous, not a doubt of it. And she hated John.

VI

For several months I heard nothing from John, which considering the circumstances was not strange, although he was always a good correspondent and endowed with literary gifts peculiar in a soldier.

One day from a mutual friend I learnt that he had bought a house in Bournemouth.

"Did you meet his wife?" I asked.

"No. She was seedy or something. But I met the mother, terrible old Tartar! Why the deuce Travers puts up with her I don't know. But he seems to like her. What's wrong with her? Drink?"

I explained that I knew nothing and had only once met the lady.

"Well, there's something wrong, I'll take my oath. If it isn't drink, it's worse. There's something uncanny about the old girl that gives one the creeps."

Singular words from a man just out of the trenches.

From this friend I obtained John's address and wrote him a short note enquiring as to his health and happiness.

It was a month before I received this reply:

THE WHITE COTTAGE,
ALUM CHINE,
BOURNEMOUTH.

MY DEAR OLD CHAP,

It is most remiss of me not to have written to you, but I must plead sheer laziness. I seem to be growing lazier every day. Whether it is the sea air or what, but one day follows another, and nothing done.

You will have wondered about us, I expect. Well, things are not all they should be. Muriel is always ill, and spends most of her time in bed. Nothing tangible. She seems to be suffering from some sort of strange, insidious disease, sleeping or sleepy sickness or something of that kind. We have had in several medicos, but they do her no good and seem as puzzled as I am—although they don't say so.

My mother-in-law is with us, doing the housekeeping, nursing Muriel, and generally running the show. The old lady is wonderful! What we should do without her I don't know. She is really rather a marvellous person, most intellectual and uncommonly amusing. Why she never married again I can't imagine. Some one missed a good wife.

Helga—I call her Helga—has also (this will surprise you) the gift of healing. This lies, she tells me, in her hands. She has always had it. Her hands are wonderful, strong and yet completely soothing.

You will be sceptical about this, I know. But I have lived too long in the East not to realise that there are certain people who are born with this healing power. Even the Bible mentions the laying on of hands. Anyhow, my head has improved enormously under her treatment. She seems literally to stroke away the pain. I have quite given up medicos and medicine.

Some news of an intimate and to the reader scarcely interesting nature followed. And the letter concluded with an invitation to run down and spend a week-end with them.

This letter caused me some uneasiness. John's affairs were not shaping well. The ill-health of his wife and the presence of the mother-in-law, though natural enough in the circumstances, seemed in my bachelor eyes altogether wrong. Matrimony was made essentially for two. Nor did I like the "stroking" that John found so soothing. It might merely be massage. But from the first, as I say, I was suspicious of Helga Stourcross.

VII

At this time I was almost exclusively occupied in war work, and week-ends were not to be thought of. And, truth to tell, the war and its victims occupied my whole mind to the exclusion of almost everything else. In those days even one's best friend was in danger of being forgotten.

I doubt whether I should have found time to think again about Travers and his troubles, which after all were as nothing to the troubles I was hourly attending to, and he at least was safe at home, had it not been for the arrival of a telegram which read:

> "Muriel seriously ill think mental for God's sake come at once John."

That was a message for help that could not be ignored.

Fortunately it was a Saturday morning. On my way to the hospital I wired John to expect me that night.

VIII

Helga Stourcross herself opened the door to me. Why, I do not pretend to know, as one at least of the maids was in. As usual she was the Queen of Tragedy. "My poor girl! My poor girl!" was her salutation as she pulled the black shawl about her and hurried me upstairs and into the sick-room without even the formality of shaking hands.

Only one gas-jet was alight and that turned very low. I turned it up and lit another.

John was nowhere to be seen. Quite unlike John, I thought. Why was he not here with his wife?

"He has one of his bad heads," said Mrs Stourcross, as if in answer to my thoughts.

I walked over to the bed. My patient was lying very still, golden hair floating over the pillows and one white arm lying limp on the quilt. Her face was turned towards the window, whose blinds were undrawn.

"Poor darling, she likes to look out of the window," came from my elbow. The woman was positively uncanny.

"Is she asleep?" I asked. For there was no movement from the bed.

"She is always like this," said Helga, "except when she has one of her storms, and then she raves and makes the most awful accusations against poor me."

"Delusions, of course?" I suggested, trying to conceal my antipathy.

"Her poor father died of drink. He was once in an asylum."

"Then you should never have allowed her to get married," I said shortly.

Helga looked at me fixedly. The almost irresistible impulse came to me to avoid her eyes, as one would avoid something unpleasant. Conquering the weakness I returned look for look as though she had been a tigress and I an unarmed hunter—the simile leapt into my mind.

I do not know how long we stood thus. Her eyes, malevolent and gleaming, positively blazed into mine. If there is madness here, I thought, you are the patient. And with all the force of long practice I kept my eyes immovably upon hers.

It was a struggle of will power. She, too, had the power of concentration. No insanity here, came the conviction; but power, enormous power, such as I had never met with. Her eyes literally burned into mine; and the hatred behind them was intense, almost overpowering.

Presently the flames in them began to burn out. The pupils gradually grew smaller. With a shiver she turned away, and with hands that trembled now she drew the black shawl about her.

"Now," I said, "I will examine the patient—alone, if you please."

With the utmost docility she acquiesced.

When the door had closed behind her I returned to John's wife.

She was lying as before, white and motionless. I took her hand. Although her eyes were open, she made no movement. The pulse was scarcely perceptible. I leant over her. The eyes, very beautiful, as I have said, were open, but seemed not to see.

"Don't you know me?" I asked. "I am John's friend, best man at your wedding, your friend, here to do all I can to help you."

She made no sign of recognition.

I applied the stethoscope to the heart, and found it beating slowly but regularly.

The girl seemed in a trance. Was it encephalitis lethargica? Somehow I doubted it.

"Don't you know me? I'm John's friend," I repeated. "John. John who loves you, who telegraphed for me to come and make you better. John, your husband."

Still no sign of awaking intelligence, and yet she was awake, for at every mention of John's name the pale lips trembled as the petals of a rose might do when stirred by a soft wind.

For some time I worked at her, with suggestion, with massage. I even took cold water from the jug and splashed her with it.

She merely shivered.

I found my way downstairs and in the hall met the maid. "Where is your master?" I asked.

"In the study, sir," she replied. "He has one of his bad heads and is not to be disturbed."

"Show me in," I said.

The girl hesitated before a door.

"Is that the room?" I asked.

"Yes, sir. And—perhaps you had best go in alone, sir. The mistress is there."

I turned the handle. The door was locked.

I knocked loudly.

There was a rustling of silk. Voices murmured. Then the voice of Mrs Stourcross enquired who was there.

I banged the door again. "It is I, Toogood. Are you there, John? I want you at once. Open the door."

The key turned. Mrs Stourcross, finger to mouth, faced me. "Hush," she murmured. "He is asleep."

On the couch, wrapped in a travelling rug, was John.

"Come out of that!" I said. This seemed too much like melodrama, and was becoming irritating. Everyone in this establishment could not be suffering from suspended animation.

With a snore John sat up, rubbed his eyes like a sleepy schoolboy, and stared vacantly at me.

By the side of the couch stood a table with a decanter, two glasses, and a jug of water. I seized the jug and emptied it over him.

That woke him up. He spluttered, "Confound you! What the devil are you doing?"

I seized his shoulders and shook him. A much bigger man than I and far more muscular, he seemed as weak as a kitten and as flabby as a jellyfish. "Confound you!" was all he could gasp. "Confound you!"

"Don't hurt him! Oh, don't hurt him!" came from Mrs Stourcross.

"Hurt him? I will shake the life out of him," I said, thoroughly angry. "There's his wife ill upstairs and waiting for him, and here he is as drunk as a sot."

"He isn't drunk," she pleaded. "It's his head, his poor head."

"Muriel wants you," I said to him sternly. "Up you come this instant."

"Muriel wants me? Muriel?" He passed a hand over his forehead. "Muriel?—my wife?—wants me. I thought she hated me. Doesn't Muriel hate me, Helga?"

"Damned nonsense! She loves you and is waiting for you. Now, up you come." And I seized his arm.

Mechanically he came with me. Helga made to come also, but I waved her back. Without a word she went. "You are to stay down-stairs until I say so," I ordered.

"Very well," she replied. "But I would like to know by whose authority you give orders in this house?"

"By John's," I answered. "Isn't that so, John?"

"I suppose so," said John weakly. "You're Toogood, aren't you? I thought so. Toogood? Toogood? I'll place you presently. It's my head, you know—this confounded wound—makes me forget my own name sometimes. I will remember presently. What do you want me to do?"

"Play the man," I said.

"All right. Give me time. Give me time. It's this— Why, it's Tom!"

Recognition leapt to his face. On the instant, almost miraculously, he became the old John. All weakness vanished. With a grasp of iron he seized my hand and wrung it nearly off. "Tom! Tom! old chap, I am delighted to see you! I knew that you would come if you could. Tom! my dear old chap, this is splendid. We are in great trouble here, Tom. Muriel, you know, my wife, is mad, I think, Tom. And I—I— sometimes I feel that I am going that way myself. It's this damned head, you know. And Muriel's is hereditary. A precious pair, Tom. What we would do without Helga, I don't know. Where's Helga? Helga!"

"She is where she is going to stay," I said. "Now, just you do what I tell you and ask no questions. Implicit obedience is the order of the day, and I am the skipper. The issue may be vital."

"Not dying? Muriel is not dying, is she?"

"No. And provided you do exactly what I tell you, she won't die. But both she and you are in grave danger."

IX

We found the patient in the same comatose condition. She appeared not to have moved so much as a finger. And the eyes still gazed vacantly towards the window.

John tip-toed to the bed. "She is bad, isn't she?" he whispered. "Hadn't we better send for Helga? She wakes up for her."

"We will see if she won't wake up for us," I said. "Now take your wife's hand and talk to her as you would have done a week after the wedding. As it is, you have only been married seven months and it should not be difficult. Go ahead, never mind me."

John hesitated.

"Go ahead," I ordered. "Surely to goodness you love your wife."

"Ye-es. But it is rather like making love to the Venus de Milo."

"But isn't it worth while if Venus comes to life? I tell you it is the only chance. If Love will not awaken her nothing will."

"God knows I love her well enough," groaned John. "The trouble is that she has no use for me. She is incapable of feeling. Helga says so. Her father—"

"Died of drink and all that sort of thing. Infernal gibberish! Don't I spend half my time dealing with that sort of confounded nonsense? There is only one trouble in this house. But I will enter into that later. Forget Helga, everything that she has ever said. Remember only the wife who adores you, who is in grave danger, and who sadly wants your help. For ten minutes let her be your Sleeping Princess. I ask you to play the Fairy Prince, as we did when we were boys—for ten minutes only."

That touched him, as I knew it would. For John was the largest-hearted of any man that I ever knew.

As he knelt down by the bed I turned the light low, and walked to the window, and opened it wide.

It was a night laden with loveliness. The May moon, but recently risen, had transformed the misty night. There were no stars, no land, no wind. The sea seemed to have melted away. Between sky and sea was no line of demarcation. Divisions had ceased; forms had faded. As far as the eye could see the whole world was one shimmering mass of a gossamer substance that shone like silver. A night to stir the soul and lift thought to its highest level.

Behind me I could hear John's whisperings, which rising once in a while shaped themselves into endearing words.

Was Love there? Knowing John as I did, I fancied so.

Silently I prayed into the silver night.

I was always a believer in prayer; no intelligent man can be otherwise. Not the "oft-repeated" words of church usage, but the lofty thought of one soul wishing another's weal. Bachelor though I am, unused as I am to love in its accepted sense, yet I have always been convinced that Love is the only form of prayer that can change the order of things as accepted by us as natural.

While Scientist and Chemist make study of the actions and reactions of one substance upon another, I have always conceived it to be the business of the Psychologist to study the actions and reactions of one law upon another. And for many years I had been searching closely into what has always been deemed the *unnatural*, that is to say, the action of such illusive and withal such powerful Laws as Love and Hate when in contact with *natural* laws.

On more than one occasion I have seen the natural course of a disease, not merely mental, but physical, altered by the presence of one or other of these two invisible agencies. Had I a patient in a precarious condition I would no more dream of permitting an evil-wisher into his presence than I would a cholera germ. This may seem drastic. Many nurses, whose tender hearts outrun their heads, many relatives of my patients, with hankerings after unearned increment, have thought me hard. No matter. I can afford, now, to do what I conceive to be my duty.

Before all the drugs on earth, before all the bottled medicine, before skilled nursing, fresh air, or sunshine, I would, and I could, let Love into the sick-room and leave him there to work his miracles. But this Elixir of Life is of so rare an occurrence that one seldom has the opportunity of using it.

Presently a woman's voice broke into my reverie. I turned. In the dim light I could see a white figure with floating hair sitting up in the bed.

"Oh, John! dear John! is it really you?" she was saying. "I thought that you were dead. Aren't you dead? Is it really you, your own self, not just a shadow in the moonlight? Oh, dear God! thank you, dear God! I thought that John was dead. And I wanted to die, too, to go and look for him. Thank you, dear God, for sending me back my love."

Love was here. The charm had worked.

There came from John a deep sound, very like a sob.

I turned once more to the window.

X

A good half-hour must have passed. The whispering from the bed had sunk into silence, when there came a knock at the door, which I had locked.

I turned and lit the light.

John's wife, with her husband's head pillowed on her breast, was stroking his hair. A most charming picture they made. A soft colour suffused her face as she saw me in the unexpected light. But she made no effort to move her posture, and it was plain that the knocking had not disturbed her. John, with eyes shut, seemed asleep.

"It is nice to see you again, Doctor Toogood," she said in her soft voice. "I hope everything is comfortable in your room. But mother will have seen to that." I thought I detected a certain bitterness in the last words, but that she was completely herself again and blissfully happy was obvious.

Again came the knocking at the door, this time loud and prolonged. The happiness faded from her face.

"Who is it?" I called sharply.

"It is I," answered the voice of Helga. "What are you doing in there to my poor girl? Open the door immediately. I won't have my girl locked into bedrooms with strange men. Where is John? John! John!" Her voice rose to a pitch that reminded me of a quarrelling fishwife.

Almost instantly John opened his eyes and jumped to his feet. As though half dazed, he looked around him, blinked at the light, then at me, then at his wife.

"John! John!" came the strident voice, accompanied by more thumps.

"Coming," he said; and went to the door, fumbling at the handle.

"It's mother," whispered Muriel. Then with sudden spirit: "Let her come in. Yes, let her in, Doctor Toogood. I am not afraid now. And it is better to get it over."

I called to John that the door was locked. Still fumbling, he opened it. And in walked Helga.

"You seem to have been having quite a session," she said. "And I see my poor darling is awake. You look cold, darling. Let me get you your bed-jacket." She approached the bed.

"I want nothing from you," said John's wife, waving her away.

"Ungrateful! Ungrateful! And all that I have done for you. You can see for yourself, Doctor, that she isn't normal. Her poor father—"

"Stop that," I said sharply. "We are having no more melodrama here. If you cannot behave as you should in a sick-room, I must ask you to go."

"She is *my* daughter," she said, eyes flashing.

"She is my *patient*," I replied.

"John!" She turned to face him. "Are you going to allow this man to insult me in my own house?"

"It is *my* house," said John's wife. The statue had certainly come to life. "Please shut the door, John. Now"—turning to her mother—"I am going to speak plainly."

And then she began her extraordinary story, which to me at that time was very nearly incredible; although, as I say, I am used to the incredible and never lightly dismiss anything because of its incredibility.

Fifty years ago, nay less, a man depicting the marvels of modern science would by the unintelligent have been called insane. And have not all the world's great visionaries been dismissed in their day as mad?

"I must tell you," commenced John's wife in quiet, level tones, "that my mother is a most remarkable woman. She is far cleverer than most men, has travelled tremendously, and can speak I don't know how many languages. A mother to be proud of, you might think. But she is—all wrong."

Helga Stourcross' face was a study.

"For years—ever since I can remember—she has made a study of the supernatural. I was brought up in an atmosphere of spiritualism, occultism, and all those hateful things. Every Sunday evening we had a séance. When I was only twelve she began to hypnotise me."

"You wicked girl! You wicked, wicked girl! How can you tell such abominable lies about your poor mother? You can see for yourself, Doctor—"

"Kindly keep quiet, or I shall be obliged to put you out," I said.

"She hypnotises John"—John blinked stupidly—"under the pretence of curing his headaches.

"Not only is she a Hypnotist, but a most powerful medium. Not only can she tell what is going to happen, but she *makes things happen*: I've seen her—hundreds of times."

"You wicked—"

"Another word, and out you go!" I said, taking her arm in no gentle grip.

"You can't imagine how I longed to get away from it all.

"I thought John would have taken me away. But he likes her—now.

"I am not ill really; only starving for fresh air and sunlight and flowers and birds and little things like that. It is my mother who is killing me; and I can't get away from her. Oh, God! why can't I get away? Oh, John! Why can't you see? Why can't you *see*?"

She sank back as it seemed exhausted. Then, with an effort, raised herself again.

"Tell me," she cried, looking at me, "do you believe in witches, Doctor Toogood?"

At this question I was somewhat taken aback and had no answer ready.

"You don't, of course; who does to-day? You don't believe what I am telling you. No one does. You only shake your head and think me mad. I am used to that. John thinks me mad. He does. He can't say no.

"But I am not mad. Sometimes I wish I were.

"You don't believe in witches, Doctor Toogood? I can show you one, my mother. Ask her. She is proud of it; glories in her power. And she has power, tremendous, awful power. I told you she could makes things happen. Things happen? Why, she can *kill* people. She killed my father. She killed my little dog—because he didn't like her and used to growl. She killed a little boy with whom I used to play. She—has killed—ever so many people. She—does not—kill them—by—in—the—ordinary way."

The words came wearily. An excessive languor seemed to be coming over her. The last vestige of colour had left her cheeks. The eyelids, I saw, were drooping. Slowly her head sank back upon the pillow.

Then the lips moved once more. "She—does—it—" The words died away. Sleep had conquered her delusions.

Poor child. Poor John.

Had I been asked then and there to sign a certificate of insanity I might—there was a time that I would—have done so. Nine out of ten, nay, ninety-nine out of a hundred medical men would there and then have certified her as suffering from delusions.

But I have learnt through long experience not to make hasty judgments, and my ideas of insanity, though they are deemed "peculiar" by the majority of my confrères, are at least listened to—now. It is so easy to certify. A scratch of the pen, and the thing is done. A thing that can never be wholly undone, and always leaves some stigma. A hasty judgment, a scratch of the pen: and many a splendid soul, many a genius has been condemned to oblivion merely because their ideas were out of the ordinary.

I have seen scores of men and women in our asylums far more intelligent and of far more service to the State than those sane people who have charge of them and who put them away.

John's wife might be mad; her utterances seemed to indicate it. On the other hand, she might not.

On an impulse I turned to the mother, whose arm I had in my interest loosed. Her face was set. The trap-like mouth tightly compressed. And the eyes, glittering and baleful, were fixed upon her daughter in that stare that I had found so peculiarly unpleasant.

"Stop that!" I said.

"Stop what? What am I accused of now?"

"Of deliberately hypnotising your daughter and sending her to sleep by suggestion," I said.

Helga Stourcross laughed. "What powers you give me, Doctor! You will be making John nervous next. Poor child! Is she really asleep?"

"Fast asleep," said John.

"Then I will tuck her up. There, there! Now you will sleep soundly, my precious, precious darling. God bless and keep you, my own; and may He take away all those terrible notions about your poor mother. There, there!

"And now for supper. It has been waiting for some time; fortunately it is cold. Come, Doctor. Your arm, John, dear."

She turned the lights low, tip-toed out of the room, and softly closed the door.

A remarkable woman, I decided as I followed them downstairs; and without doubt a very powerful hypnotist. There was a very great deal more in this house than met the eye.

XI

At supper Helga Stourcross was as brilliant as the meal was excellent. She certainly believed not only "in feeding the brute" but in keeping him amused. As a society hostess she would have shone.

From her manner, not only had she forgiven, but completely forgotten, all that had taken place. Not once did she allude to her daughter upstairs. To charm was her intention. That she failed to charm me that night was through no fault of her own, but because of that repugnance that I had conceived for her from the first moment of our meeting.

Many men view instinctive likes and dislikes with suspicion. Most women rely upon them, it is said, unreasonably. Not so. In this respect women display far more reason than men. For there is not the least doubt but what Intuition is the voice of Nature informing us of the existence of a Law, one of the first laws of creation, that of Attraction and Repulsion; which Science has discovered responsible, on the physical plane, for all material motion, and which Psychology is discovering responsible, on the psychic or occult plane, for all spiritual movement.

If I conceive an immediate dislike for a person, I know that there is some quality in that person's character that is inimical to some quality in my own. Friendship with that person is not good for me; not good for the growth of my character, or what is commonly termed my spiritual well-being. I do not say that we cannot, or should not, overcome this natural repulsion. But I do say that they should be accepted, reasonably accepted, as warnings to walk very warily.

Charm she never so cleverly, Helga Stourcross was to me suspect, without taking into consideration the recent utterances of her daughter, which might, or might not, be the delusions of a woman suffering from some form of insanity.

John, on the other hand, was her devoted slave. He hung on her words as if they had been jewels. He laughed uproariously at her satirical, and certainly witty, sallies. He might have been her husband, not the husband of the poor girl upstairs. Frankly, I was disgusted with him.

The more I watched him, the more I realised how great was the change that had come over him. At all times the most abstemious of men, now he was drinking considerably more than was good for him. And it was Mrs Stourcross who filled his glass. Of a studious, almost mystical, turn of mind, now he was giving voice to sentiments bordering upon the lewd, sentiments that made me ashamed for him, and which Mrs Stourcross enjoyed with evident relish.

A brilliant and evil-minded woman who would be a danger to all who associated with her, I decided. And the words: "She hypnotises him," returned again and again to my mind.

Was she really a Hypnotist in the accepted sense? or was it merely the force of a powerful personality that made itself felt by those immediately surrounding her? Was she, in short, a conscious or unconscious Hypnotist? Did she know her power? For power she had. I could feel it myself. With my mind's eye I could almost *see* it radiating from her as radium radiates under the microscope. Undoubtedly she was hypnotising her daughter. Had she the same power over John?

It certainly appeared so. An evil and dangerous woman.

XII

After supper I suggested a visit to the patient.

"She will be sleeping," said Mrs Stourcross sweetly.

"She must have food," I insisted.

"She will have her milk and brandy at twelve as Doctor Mikhaïlovitch ordered. A very clever man, isn't he, John?"

John agreed.

"Will she be awake then?" I asked.

"Oh, yes, she is most regular, isn't she, John?" John nodded.

"And who will give it her?"

"I will, of course. Don't think for a moment, Doctor Toogood, that my poor darling lacks attention. I love looking after her, don't I, John?"

Again John agreed.

The man had become her echo. How on earth he had come to send me that telegram I could not for the life of me imagine. It must have been during some moment when he was free of her influence. Was he afraid of her? He did not seem to be. Rather he appeared devoted to her and ready to acquiesce in her every wish and to agree with her every word.

"By the way, Doctor Mikhaïlovitch is coming to-morrow at ten, isn't he, John? Won't that be a little awkward for you, Doctor Toogood?"

"Not in the least," I said. "You are quite entitled to another opinion. I take it," I turned to John, "that Doctor Mikhaïlovitch was consulted before that wire was sent to me?"

"What wire? I sent you no wire, Doctor Toogood. Did I, John?"

"No. But John did," I said.

"Did you send Doctor Toogood a wire, John?"

"Wire? Toogood? Why should I wire Toogood?"

"Don't lie, man," I said, thoroughly angry. "You know you wired for me. I have the telegram here. And you know," and I turned to Mrs Stourcross, "that you expected me. Didn't you open the door to me yourself? Didn't you show me into your daughter's room?"

She smiled sweetly. "I am afraid there is some mistake, somewhere, probably mine. We have been very worried lately, haven't we, John? John never intended to call you in in a professional capacity, did you, John? And I—I thought you might like to see my poor girl as a friend, merely as a friend, Doctor Toogood. I am quite sure Doctor Mikhaïlovitch was not consulted, was he, John?

"So you see it is rather awkward, isn't it? For although we love to have you as a friend, we are perfectly satisfied with Doctor Mikhaïlovitch as a doctor, aren't we, John?"

"Perfectly," echoed John.

What a consummate actress the woman was! And what a liar! Had she been a man I should probably have done something drastic. For there are men to whom one may talk with the tongue of angels but who only understand the language of force. It is the one language they understand and respect. To them a fist full in the mouth is far more convincing than a whole series of learned arguments. Never yet did pearls agree with swine. A fact that may seem pathetic to the unbalanced sentimentalist, but a fact nevertheless. Unfortunately I was dealing with a woman. With a woman one smiles.

I smiled now. "Very good indeed," I said. "Mrs Stourcross, I congratulate you. On the stage you would have been superb."

"Do you think so?" She gave me smile for smile.

"I am certain of it. As I am certain that you are a most remarkable Hypnotist."

"How interesting! When I was quite a girl I remember being told by a spiritualist friend that I had all the qualities of a medium. He wanted me to sit for him." She laughed. "But I thought it too dangerous. It is dangerous, isn't it, Doctor Toogood?"

"Very," I said.

"That is what Doctor Mikhaïlovitch says. He is wonderful at it. For some time now he has been hypnotising John for his head-aches. He takes them quite away, doesn't he, John? And recently he has been treating Muriel in the same way. He is also a very clever Psycho-Analyst, although personally I think him rather too fond of sex questions. He is rather Freudian for my taste."

"Is that so?" I said. "I shall indeed be pleased to meet him to-morrow."

"So you see," she smiled archly, "you were right in a way, and in a way wrong. You thought that John and Muriel were both being hypno-tised; which was very clever of you, wasn't it, John? But you thought that I was doing it. I wish I could. For then I might make my poor girl better. A mother's love, Doctor Toogood, is so wonderful, isn't it?

"Poor child! Doctor Mikhaïlovitch holds out little hope. In his opinion she is quite wanting, and he is trying to persuade us to send her to a mental home, isn't he, John? But I couldn't bear to think of my poor girl shut up away from those who love her. She is my only one, my own ewe lamb, Doctor Toogood. You can understand my feelings." Tears streamed down her cheeks.

Had I misjudged her after all? What possible motive could she have in wishing to harm her own daughter? What possible motive in wishing to harm John? Perhaps—"

"And now I come to think of it," the voice of Mrs Stourcross interrupted my thoughts, "John must have sent that telegram after

Doctor Mikhaïlovitch's last visit. He was very insistent on getting her into a home, and John was naturally most upset. Was that when you sent it, John?"

Like an automaton John nodded.

As I saw him thus, nodding stupidly, I remembered, in a flash, the man he had been. Who was to blame for his present condition? Himself? or Helga Stourcross? or this tinkering Hypnotist, Mikhaïlovitch?

And the girl upstairs? Who was to blame for that feeble wreck who should have been a splendid woman? Was this Russian, of whom one had never even heard, subtly instilling, by means of psycho-analysis, the poison of his own soul into these unfortunate people? It would be a great pleasure to interview friend Mikhaïlovitch in the morning.

Here was a household that ought to be perfectly happy, that had all the ingredients of happiness within its grasp, that was intended, created for happiness. And yet it was worse than many a slum tenement. Only one member of it seemed to be happy, and that Helga Stourcross.

She was happy, not a doubt of it. Why?

"I am going up now to see my darling child. Would you care to accompany me, Doctor Toogood?"

"As a friend?"

"That would be very nice. You, John, will go to bed, I suppose."

"I suppose so," said John.

On the way upstairs Helga Stourcross halted and turned to me. "Your arm, Doctor Toogood. These stairs are very trying."

As her hand touched my arm I felt a thrill as from a live wire.

XIII

We found the patient apparently still sound asleep. Her eyes were shut, and both breathing and pulse normal. Mrs Stourcross tucked her up as though she had been a baby, kissed her tenderly, assured me that she would awake at midnight for her food, and accompanied me to my room. There she made sure that everything was as it should be, and hoped that I would sleep well. She, of course, would not sleep, but would put on a dressing-gown and sit up with her poor darling. John slept upstairs, as he was a light sleeper and disturbed nights were not good for him. Breakfast was at nine-thirty on Sundays. The maid would call me at eight-thirty. Of course, I liked morning tea. And would I care for a nightcap?

I accepted the morning tea, declined the nightcap, and bade her good night.

As a rule I am a good sleeper, for it has been part of my self training at night to shut out assiduously from my mind all sleep-destroying thoughts. Sufficient unto the day are the problems thereof, has been my motto: and in my own case at any rate no good has ever come of midnight decisions, which by daylight generally present a different aspect from what they did in the dark.

Now, in spite of my determination, in spite of the fact that I was dog-tired, in spite of the most comfortable bed, I could not sleep. Hour after hour passed; and as religiously as I turned them back thoughts of Helga Stourcross would return. It was as though I were being attacked by mental wasps, who the more I drove them away the more viciously returned to the attack. At length will triumphed and I fell asleep: to dream that Mrs Stourcross was a saint and I the most violent of her persecutors.

It was with this impression on my mind that I awoke to the maid's knocking. And this impression in a somewhat modified form remained with me until I was seated in the train that was to take me back to Town. Then and only then did I begin to question its truth. I recalled my first intuitive idea of her as a very dangerous woman. How had my judgment become so warped in so short a time? Had I, too, fallen under the spell of her tremendous personality?

It certainly seemed like it. Had not I, who disliked the vain repetition of Church Services, and never took part in them, submitted to being taken to church by Mrs Stourcross as meekly as John had submitted? Had I not accepted her explanation that Doctor Mikhaïlovitch had telephoned to say that an urgent case had called him into the country and that he would be round in the evening at eight-thirty instead of in the morning? Indeed, I had made not the slightest attempt to verify this statement. I had even neglected to procure Doctor Mikhaïlovitch's address. And had I not almost come to like this woman and to believe in her?

It seemed that she had almost forced me to accept her at her own valuation: that of a most religious and good woman wrestling nobly with very cruel circumstances.

"What would we do without her?" John had said after lunch.

And I myself had answered: "What indeed?"

Poor John! A fine friend I had proved myself. Knowing him as I did, his thoughts, aspirations, and character—the very soul and substance of him; and loving him for them, as I did, to have allowed myself to be persuaded that that weak, dissolute, unworthy specimen of humanity masquerading in his body was him, John Travers.

John? It was no more him than a faded and badly taken photograph would have been. An unpleasant caricature only; a caricature drawn by—Helga Stourcross.

And Muriel, his wife? She, too, was a mere shell, out of which all personality, all the soul had been drained by—Helga Stourcross.

Not quite all. There was yet some spirit latent, that John's love had called to life. A flicker that had soon gone out under the gaze of—Helga Stourcross.

I myself? Were my nerves, too, suffering from overwork? I had certainly not been myself in that house. Undoubtedly not. I had behaved like a weak, credulous idiot. I had been persuaded into false judgments; into misjudging my best friend; almost into disliking my best friend; almost into liking for a woman whom I knew, now that I was away from her, to be thoroughly evil.

What a personality, what power, the woman had! John's personality was strong; and she had completely subjugated it. Mine, too, was strong. What would she have made of me in a month—a year?

XIV

One of the first things I did upon reaching home was to turn to the Medical Directory and look up the name Mikhaïlovitch. It was not there. Later I sent for a copy of the Bournemouth and District Telephone Directory. No such person was on the telephone.

By this time I had come to the conclusion that the only hope for Travers and his wife was to get away from Helga Stourcross' sinister influence. For they could of their own volition no more leave her than a moth could leave the light or the steel the magnet that holds it fast.

How to get them away, that was the question.

It was a perplexing problem. Turn and twist it as I would no solution presented itself. It seemed that I could do nothing. My invitation to Travers to come up and pay me a visit met with a polite refusal. Muriel, though better, was still confined to her room, and he could not possibly leave her.

The notion came to me that I might be able to get her removed, temporarily, to my own mental home and so away from her mother. I felt sure that she would then improve almost immediately. But how to obtain Travers' consent when he himself was under the same mental thraldom?

I wrote making the suggestion; to be answered by Helga Stourcross herself in the following strain:

DEAR DOCTOR TOOGOOD,

Your most *extraordinary* letter received by John this morning. He has asked me to reply to it, as he is suffering from one of his *appalling* heads, poor boy.

Your suggestion that Muriel should be sent to an Asylum *hurt* me *very much*. Who could possibly be expected to look after her *better* than her *own mother?* who *loves* her and sits up with her night after night.

God knows I am used to being misunderstood. But at least I should have thought that *you*, with your experience, would have understood the *power* of mother-love. That alone, I am sure, stands between my poor darling and the grave. Her poor father died when he was only thirty, and there is consumption in the family.

As a matter of fact, Muriel is very much better. She is sitting up now by a nice warm fire and her appetite is quite good. I am hoping to have her downstairs to-morrow. And if the weather improves there is no reason why she should not go out after a day or two in a *bath chair*.

With love from John and the kindest regards from myself,
                                           Yours affectionately,
                                    HELGA STOURCROSS.

P.S.—Doctor Mikhaïlovitch was obliged to return to Vienna last week. We miss him dreadfully. He was quite *wonderful*.

I think there is too *much* psychoanalysis and auto-suggestion nowadays, don't you?

XV

Were it not for that mystical Something which weaves the pattern of our lives, called Fate, or Destiny, by some, by others God, most of us would spend our lives in the first deep rut that crosses our way of life. But these ruts are only obstacles in the race. Seldom do we die in that first ditch. Unseen hands take us out of it if we are too tired to listen to the urging of the unheard voice.

Travers was now in one of these ruts, an abysmal one, out of which there seemed no means of helping him; out of which he could not help himself. I, puzzle and perplex myself as I would, could see no way out. But I have learned, after many years, to trust "this scheme of things" that is not so "sorry" as at first sight it seems. I waited now; and in my own way prayed for help for these unfortunate people.

The solution came simply enough. Travers was passed fit for light duty at his next medical board and was given a billet at the India Office.

Now was my chance to help him. Not if I could possibly help it would the Bournemouth *ménage* be repeated in London. To get away from Helga Stourcross' influence was essential for him. Immediately I wrote begging him to keep a lonely old bachelor company.

Mrs Stourcross' reply was a masterpiece of vituperation—against the Government, the medical authorities, the Army Council, against everyone and everything that could have been in the slightest degree suspected of having passed John fit for service and so broken up her happy home. Her happy home!

"It's *cruel*, CRUEL, CRUEL!!" she wrote. "Hasn't *he* done *enough*? And my poor girl dying by inches! I suppose they want him to be *killed*, to avoid paying his PENSION. Why don't they take the Conscientious Objectors? Surely there are enough of *them*, and *they* wouldn't be missed. But *they* prefer to rob *widows* and *orphans*! That's like them. They *know* they have only WEAK WOMEN to deal with. Oh! for a *man*, a CROMWELL! Why does *God* allow it all?"

There were six scrawled, dashed, and smeared pages of it, which breathed, if ever writing did, most malevolent hatred of anything and everything in any way opposed to her own plans.

I confess that this unreasoning exhibition of hate amused me at the time. Not so the postscript, which was to the effect that as John could not possibly leave his wife, they were letting the house in Bournemouth and taking Furnished Apartments in the neighbourhood of Westminster, close to John's work. "So kind of you to think of him," she concluded. "But, of course, he could no more dream of leaving poor Muriel than I could."

Checkmate, I thought; certainly to my move. A woman hysterical perhaps, but of amazing intellect and courage, who would think nothing of sitting down to a game of Beggar-My-Neighbour with the Devil.

XVI

My next news was that they were installed in Cowley Street, a back street not far from the Houses of Parliament.

There one evening I went to see them—"as a friend," I explained to Mrs Stourcross, who seemed actually pleased to see me. She appeared to be in the Seventh Heaven. Unpainted, ill-lighted, unattractive, the house of their habitation was apologised for as "old-fashioned and very handy for John's work." The rooms, which to me looked paltry, dusty, poorly furnished, and lighted only by evil-smelling and certainly old-fashioned oil lamps, were pronounced "most comfy." Even the landlady, a sour-visaged person of a very low type, and her daughter, a pimply girl plastered with powder and liberally covered with tin trinkets, were "angels."

Poor John. It seemed that Fate had dragged him from his ditch only to let him fall into this morass. How he could stand it; how his wife, how Helga Stourcross herself, could stand it, was beyond me.

But I soon saw that in spite of the changed surroundings the situation was unchanged.

As assuredly as though the dwellers in some city slum suddenly transported, curses, bedding, brawling brats, and bird-cages into the Kingdom of Heaven, would make a new slum there, and, inversely, as assuredly as the inhabitants of some far-off Heaven suddenly pitched into the meanest of our streets would make of it a Heaven, so had Helga Stourcross made of Number – Cowley Street, a New Hospital.

Muriel was still upstairs and still in bed. "A relapse after the trying move," as Helga Stourcross explained.

John was still lying down, in a smaller room, on another sofa, with another table by his side on which stood other—or was it the same?—decanter and glasses, his legs covered by the same—or was it another?—travelling rug.

"Is that the way you serve your country?" I asked him. "Lolling about like an idiot and swilling that stuff? I expected to see you up and doing. Stand up and shake hands, man, like a man."

John smiled weakly. "All right for you to talk," he said. "But I'm feeling rotten. These heads," he stroked the place where his wound had been, "oh, God, these heads! I sometimes think I'm going mad. Am I mad, Tom? You ought to know. Am I mad?"

"Mad? Nothing of the sort! You're lazy, bone lazy, that's the matter. If I had been on your Board I would have sent you out to France. You want to get away from all these women; away from yourself and your paltry ailments. Heavens, man, isn't there enough man's work to do without fooling away your time like this?"

"I wasn't always like this," he groaned. "I used to be a man once. But now—oh, God! oh, God!"

"Poor boy! poor boy!" Helga Stourcross was at his side—I had thought her in the other room—stroking his hands, his head, fondling him as though he had been her child. Then, like an enraged tigress she turned on me, eyes blazing, face empty of all semblance of goodwill. "A nice doctor, you! If you were the only doctor on earth you wouldn't touch him. Leave this house at once. Do you hear me? Leave this house at once."

"Very well," I said. "If John says so."

"Tell him to go, John," she ordered instantly.

"I think you had better go," said John.

"Right," I replied. What else could I reply? Had I been a brick-layer I might have cuffed or kicked her. She would have understood that, and respected it and the bricklayer. And it would have done her a deal of good—no doubt. As it was, my fingers itched to take her by the shoulders and give her a good shaking. Had she, by some colossal mischance, been my wife I would have—I don't know what I would have done. So far are women, for all their boasted equality, removed from equality.

"Good-bye, John." I held out my hand. But his were fast in hers. "Good-bye. I don't suppose I shall see you again. The sight sickens. You, a man, a man in a million, come to this; thanks to you," and I turned to Helga Stourcross. "As for you, you win, so far, hands down. You have got him, body and soul. He's yours, to drain of manhood and to destitute of courage and every other quality that goes to make a splendid soul. Suck him dry, dear Mrs Stourcross. May he do you good and not disagree with your digestion."

"Disgusting!" came from her lips. But her face showed that the shafts had struck.

"Disgusting, yes. Isn't a vampire always disgusting, more especially when in human form? Although you, dear Mrs Stourcross, are an exceptional vampire, not in the least like the common variety. You do not feed on money, but on finer stuff, the substance of men's hearts and minds, the very essence of Life itself. Good hunting, Mrs Stourcross. And when the feast is finished, remember that there is always the bill to meet."

With that I left them. And the evil smile that followed me and which I saw repeated in the pier-glass told me, more truthfully than words, that Helga Stourcross believed that I was beaten and that to her was the victory. Which was exactly what I had wanted her to believe.

XVII

G rateful patients in many instances mean friends. I had a friend at the India Office of some influence. I invited him to dine; and over the port told him the substance of what has been here set down and invited his co-operation.

Had he been a less intellectual man and less grateful, he might have laughed. As it was he believed, sympathised, and promised all the assistance in his power.

My plan was simple. As soon as possible Travers was to be re-boarded, and I was to be on the Board. The Board, under my persuasion, would do one of two things—I had not yet definitely decided which:—either Travers would be passed fit for General Service and sent out to France, or he would be ordered to my Hospital. It would depend upon his condition at the time. In either case he would be effectually removed from Helga Stourcross' influence.

A fortnight later John was boarded. I presided. Before his case came on I had explained sufficient to my two colleagues to insure their co-operation.

Owing, no doubt, to his enforced absence from his mother-in-law's ministrations during the major part of the day, John was decidedly better. He seemed very surprised to see me, shook hands cordially, and as he stood before us, held himself fairly erect and answered our questions, if not enthusiastically, at all events fairly lucidly. And as the wound in his head was quite healed, his removal to my Hospital was quite out of the question. So we passed him fit for General Service.

To Helga Stourcross it came as a veritable bombshell. Having presumably extracted from John the information that I had been on the Board, she wrote me what I can only describe as the most amazing epistle I have ever received. The first two pages consisted solely of epithets concerning my personal and professional character. I was a "sexual, immoral, unnatural, perverted monster of the Freudian order." I was "all Œdipus complex." My reputation was known from one end of London to another. "A slimy reptile," "a snake in the grass," "a noxious toad," "a sink of iniquity." Under the cloak of friendship I had "wormed my way" into her house and "stolen the affections" not only of her "dear son-in-law" but of her "darling child," her "one ewe lamb." It was "clear to everyone" that I was "in love with her daughter." I was a "robber of widows and orphans," a "disgrace to my profession" and "the name of gentleman." In short, I was a most unmitigated blackguard.

John she likened unto Uriah the Hittite.

But God would intervene on her behalf. He—underlined heavily—would not permit the wicked to triumph for ever. There would come a day of reckoning. My sin would find me out. His—underlined heavily—vengeance would fall upon me, and that very soon—the very soon underlined repeatedly—sooner than I expected. I would pay, oh! I would pay—pay—pay, to the uttermost farthing!

Meanwhile she was writing to the Medical Association, the India Office, the Army Council, the Archbishop of Canterbury, the Prime Minister, to the Queen herself. The latter, being a woman, would understand.

She signed herself: "The poor mother you have so cruelly robbed."

What she thought to gain by such a letter I could not understand, and it was scarcely in keeping with the character I had given her.

Rather it was the snarling of some semi-insane creature than the letter of a woman whom I had judged to be exceptionally strong-minded and exceedingly astute.

But the complexities of human character, more especially of the female sex, have a most expansive range.

Whether she did write to Her Majesty, the Prime Minister, the Archbishop of Canterbury, or the Army Council I do not know. It seems likely, for she certainly wrote to the India Office and the Medical Association. And I am of the opinion that in both these offices, at any rate among the junior staff, my reputation is not un-blemished. To this day among the young ladies who ply typewriters in the office of our Association I am looked upon as a gay dog.

Such is the power of slander; more especially when the slander is tinged even with the most twisted of truths and the slanderer a woman.

Had I been young and struggling and poor Helga Stourcross might have done me much material damage. Had it not been for my friend at the India Office she might have caused unpleasantness there. As it was, within the month John Travers was in France.

I wrote him as regularly as I was able. At first his replies were laconic and distinctly unfriendly. Helga Stourcross, too, was keep-ing up a regular correspondence with him, obviously. Not readily would she give up her hold on him. But I persisted patiently. If it were possible I would regain John's confidence and affection, not so much for my own sake as for his.

After a time his letters became longer and more like they had been in the old days. The old spirit began to glow in them. Little by little cynicism was extinguished, the warped thoughts grew straight, poetic vision and mysticism crept back into their former place. It was as though John, my old friend, who had so long been dead, was coming back to life. And less and less did Helga's name appear in his letters.

It was obvious that my plan was working and that Helga's influence over him was on the wane. I wondered how often he was writing to her, and what she thought of his letters now. She too would be realising that she was fast losing her grip upon his soul.

More and more frequently he referred to his wife. Indeed, as time drew on and he was appointed to the Staff, and so had more leisure to write, his letters became full of her. That he still loved her devotedly was beyond doubt.

"I know that my wife is in grave danger," ran one of his letters. "I don't know why I know, but I do. Whenever I think of her, whenever I dream of her, which I often do, I see her as it were surrounded by a sort of fog, which seems to be choking out her life. I see her battle with it, choking and gasping for breath, as I have seen men over here do when caught unawares in a gas attack. I see it as it were with my mind's eye, as clearly as if I was looking at it. And all the time she is holding out her arms to me; imploring my help.

"It's hellish when one can't do anything! What does it mean? O wise necromancer, dear old chap, can you interpret my most distressing dreams? I believe that's part of the job of you Psychologists."

To this letter I replied at full length, giving him some of my ideas and deductions. The fog that he saw with his mind's eye surrounding his wife was a mental atmosphere, or aura. This mental atmosphere was just as real as a material fog, but whereas the one, being physical, was only visible to the optic nerve, the other, being psychical, was only visible to the psychic or mental eye. He saw it, with his mind's eye, as he had very rightly said, and when he thought of his wife, because by the act of thinking about her he was putting his mind in touch with hers, and so focusing his mental eye to her aura.

The same thing would happen in sleep. For sleep was Nature's anæsthetic for the physical senses and in no way ever affected the psychic senses, but rather made them more sensitive.

I further explained that telepathic vision was only possible between two minds or two souls in tune. And further, only possible when these same minds were not only in complete harmony, but actually thinking of one another at the same instant of time. Given these conditions, telepathic communication and telepathic vision were as reasonably certain as telegraphy or photography.

Referring again to the aura or mental atmosphere, I pointed out that as a general rule this was the expression of the person's mind, and varied solely in the qualities of light and shade. A gloomy-minded individual would have a gloomy aura, the light-hearted an aura of light. But there were exceptions to this rule, viz. when one person was under the hypnotic or magnetic influence of another. Then the hypnotised person's aura would appear shrouded or overshadowed by the aura of the other.

I ended by saying that this telepathic vision appeared to me to indicate that his wife was under the influence of a personality far more powerful than her own; that this personality, whether actually hypnotic or merely magnetic, was overpowering her own. She, that is her subconscious or psychic self, was conscious of this, although her physical self might be, nay, most certainly was, unaware of it. It was her spiritual self therefore that was sending out those persistent appeals to his spiritual self. Or, as a poet would put it, her soul was calling to his.

XVIII

At first John was most dubious of my ideas.

"Your letter, contents noted but only partially comprehended, gave me the most confounded headache," he wrote. "Of course, your obvious implication is that Muriel's mother is a species of human vamp, the sort of person one would expect to meet in *Dracula* and not a drawing-room. My dear old chap, even supposing her to be all you suggest—which to me is inconceivable—what possible motive could she have in harming her own daughter?"—(my own thought, as I remembered). "I don't suppose that even the most vitiated of vamps would devour its own progeny. Not being a scientist, I can't say, but anyway it don't seem natural.

"No, you are on the wrong tack there. Helga, although I know you don't like her, is really a very good sort. Last week she sent me socks and all sorts of things. And the way she looks after Muriel is simply wonderful. Where would Muriel be without her now? Why, my dear old chap, my one consolation is that if anything should happen to me out here, there is always Helga.

"I wish you two could be friends. But she seems to dislike you as much as you do her. Her last letter, received by the same post as yours, positively bristled about you.

"Muriel, thank God, is better—so much for bad dreams! Her appetite has improved and she is going out in a bath chair, *which Helga pushes herself*. What a vamp, eh? My dear old chap, if you don't take care and work less, it will be a case of the patient prescribing for the doctor, what?"

In subsequent letters I was more tactful. For after all what concrete proof had I against Helga Stourcross? Of what could I accuse her? Of being in league with the Powers of Darkness? How John would have laughed at that! And had I set down in writing but a fraction of what I had deduced, he would have been justified in doubting my sanity; and thus my object would have been defeated.

The way of no pioneer is easy. That of the explorer of the uncharted realms of the Unseen is especially fraught with danger; for even the ship in which he sails is suspect. Never has a visionary, never has a mystic, escaped suspicion.

For a long time, as I say, John steadfastly declined to accept my ideas concerning his mother-in-law. "You are prejudiced," he wrote in one letter. "The first time I have found you so. Mutual antipathy, I suppose."

In another: "I can't say that I like her, for one knows that she is all wrong in her ideas. But I cannot help being sorry for her. In the back of my brain—or it may be my heart—I have a feeling that somehow she has just missed being great: that in some way or other she has got off on the wrong tack, perhaps missed her vocation; and so her character has become warped and herself miserable."

In another: "It would be utterly impossible for me to take your advice. I know that Muriel and I ought to be happy, as you say; that we were meant to be happy; that she and I together could be happy anywhere, under almost any circumstances. I love her with my head, my heart, my body. I love her with my soul, I think. And I know, without egotism, that she loves me. But I cannot persuade myself that it is right to send her mother away. It would break the old lady's heart. And somehow, in a way I cannot explain, I feel bound to her."

It was clear that Helga still retained some hold upon him, and that despite the distance that divided them.

Was it a case of Telepathic Hypnotism?

The question opened up a whole series of most interesting possibilities. For although I had never met a case of it, I had for some time past believed it to be possible. A Parsee patient of mine had once told me that in the East this power to hypnotise at a distance was not unknown, although he personally had never known anyone who could do it. The power was said to be vested in the order of Fakirs, and was by them kept a profound secret.

A prolonged investigation of what is commonly called Christian Science had led me also to believe that the "Absent Treatment," which is a conspicuous feature of this faith—if we may so describe it—is merely another form of Telepathic Hypnotism.

So great was my interest in this my first case of it—if it was it?—that I positively hankered to get into touch once more with Helga Stourcross. Never perhaps would another such opportunity come my way.

The sequel was unexpected. The very next day I received a post card, in Helga's handwriting, which read:—

> You cruel monster! How dare you try and make mischief between myself and my son-in-law! What has it got to do with *you*? Mind your *own business* and leave us to mind *ours*.
>
> I thought you were supposed to be a *Doctor*? Not a *Parson!* Yet you seem to spend your time trying to save people's *souls* by POST! What has John's *soul* to do with *you*? Look after *your* OWN. I expect it is BLACK enough.

It was signed H. S. There was no address. The postmark was Bournemouth.

This interesting epistle furnished me with further food for thought. Then I commenced a series of experiments. Regularly at a fixed hour every evening, eleven o'clock, to be exact, I gave thirty minutes' thought to John, or as a religious person would say, I prayed for him for thirty minutes every evening. The substance of my prayers was to free him from Helga's influence; to cut, as it were, the invisible connection between them.

At the same time, I kept up a regular correspondence.

Whatever the vehicle, whether the unspoken thought or the written word, it soon became apparent that I was making headway. In one letter John admitted that his picture of a post-war Heaven was "a creeper-clad cottage, somewhere in Cornwall, in sight and sound of the sea; with jasmine and honeysuckle scrambling over a little porch, and roses looking in at the windows. A cottage just for two."

Another contained the remark: "I'm d—d if we are going to inhabit any more hospitals—when I get home." Another: "As you say, it is all a matter of 'atmosphere.' We must get a healthy atmosphere about the place and clear out everything unhealthy. Helga has a most unhealthy mind, of that I feel convinced."

And then, without word or warning, John presented himself in person.

XIX

The improvement in John was amazing, and I felt more than justified in the steps I had taken. He was over on short leave he explained as he shook my hand in a grasp that lacked nothing of firmness, and had just run up from Bournemouth to see me.

"It's about Muriel," he said. "They're in two furnished rooms in Bournemouth now, abominable place, in a back street, and a most repulsive old landlady. The uglier they are the better she seems to like 'em. How in the world they ever picked such a place beats me."

"So they left Cowley Street?" I asked.

"Yes, didn't you know? From there they went to South Kensington. That was unsatisfactory and they went back to Bournemouth. Our place is let, of course, and God knows, with this Restriction Act, when we shall be able to get into it again. But the show they are in now is the limit."

"How is your wife?" I asked.

"In a bad way. Just about all in. Didn't even recognise me at first. D'you know," he knitted his brows, "I've come to the conclusion that there is a lot in what you say. There's something radically wrong with that mother-in-law of mine. She isn't normal."

"She is not," I said.

"Funny! I used to like her," he went on. "Now she gets on my nerves, makes me want to shout or to smash something. Last night we had the devil's own shindy. I wanted to see Muriel. She said I couldn't. I insisted. And she planted herself in front of the door, and said something about crossing her dead body first. I might have been a Hun from the way she treated me, and the language she used was—well, one's used to language, but this was beyond anything. A sergeant-major wasn't in it. She must have been drinking or something."

"What happened?"

"Well, I wasn't going to be browbeaten any longer. So I took her by the shoulders and shoved her aside. Scarcely the way to treat a lady. But I had put up with a lot, I can tell you. To begin with, there was no room for me in the beastly house so she and the loathsome landlady said. Muriel and her mother apparently shared a bedroom and all the others were let; and they only had one sitting-room. They suggested giving me a shakedown on the sofa. I struck; and went to an hotel. I believe in pigging it when it is necessary: not when it isn't.

"Believe me, old chap, they are living like—like paupers. God only knows why!

"No wonder Muriel is ill! Why, that damned place would kill me."

"I believe you," I said.

"D'you know last night was the first time I saw her, and I've been home five days. For five days they put me off, the two of them. I don't know why I stood it so long. But last night, oh lordy, lordy, what a shindy there was! It sounded like a Belgian atrocity."

"And what did your wife think about it?"

"At first she was dazed, didn't even know me, and kept moaning to herself like a sick child, fit to break a man's heart. After a time she seemed to wake up and implored me to save her. She seems terrified of her mother and accuses her of the most incredible things. And she believes them, that's the strange part of it. Her mind was undoubtedly wandering, poor girl.

"But I've made up my mind. I am going to take her away. She will never get better in that atmosphere."

"She will not," I agreed.

"Looking back on our married life, I see what an abject idiot I've been," continued John. "I've never even given my wife a dog's chance. She ought to have had a home of her own, not played second fiddle to her mother. Helga has always run everything. She has always been the mistress, Muriel always her daughter. And I, God knows for what reason, laziness I suppose—it seemed the easiest way—I consented to this unnatural arrangement.

"Thank God my eyes are open at last and I can see clearly for the first time since our marriage. I seem to have been living in a sort of fog; the wound in my head I expect, or neurasthenia or something. It's finished now, thank God, and I am going to take Muriel right away. That's what I've come to see you about."

"Did you tell Helga?" I asked.

"You bet I did, this morning. It seems scarcely credible, but this morning she was as mild as new milk; actually seemed to have forgotten all about last night's shindy. Tried to kiss me when I turned up, and offered me whiskey. I wasn't having any of either. Then the trouble started. She carried on like a crazy thing. Said that I was robbing her of her ewe lamb and all that sort of thing. Insisted that I would kill her daughter if I moved her. Of course the filthy old landlady backed her up. They even sent for a doctor, a greasy half-caste chap, who supported her through thick and thin."

While he had been talking I had been thinking; and had come to a conclusion.

"When is your leave up?" I asked.

"To-morrow. That's the devil of it."

"Right. Then you must bring your wife up here. I will look after her. Plenty of room, and it will be a great pleasure."

John grasped my hand in a grip that hurt. "That's just like you," he said. "The very thing, and you're the very man to put her right. And after the war," his eyes grew misty, "we'll have that little cottage by the sea with the jasmine and the honeysuckle and the roses. And you will come down for your holidays there. I love her, you know. I would give my life to make her happy."

How well I remembered those words afterwards.

So it was settled. Muriel was to come to me until after the war. John was to go back to Bournemouth and bring her up the following morning, in a taxi, if necessary in an ambulance.

"There'll be the deuce of a shindy," laughed John. "And I would sooner face a machine-gun than those two women. But we will be here by lunch-time to-morrow."

When he had left I felt certain qualms that I had not offered to accompany him. But, as usual, I had a tremendous rush of patients and could scarcely have done so.

That evening I explained the position to my housekeeper, a worthy soul who has been with me for more than twenty years. She was most sympathetic, as I knew she would be. And by lunch-time everything for the reception of our guest was in readiness.

One o'clock came, and there was no sign of her. I lingered an extra half-hour over lunch. Still they did not come.

In spite of myself I began to grow anxious. But comforted myself with the thought that the getting of an ambulance for so long a journey might have presented difficulties. In any case John's leave was up and he would have to catch the boat-train. Leaving instructions that I was to be telephoned to the moment they arrived, I went to my work.

The afternoon passed; and no message. At six o'clock I returned home. No sign of them. Not even a telegram.

By this time I had become exceedingly anxious, and a thousand and one possibilities crossed my mind.

At ten o'clock John arrived, alone, and in a state of great excitement. "She's beaten us," he burst out. "The old devil! If I could only
get my hands on her."

"What's happened?" I asked.

"Happened? They've gone, disappeared completely, leaving this."
He flung a half-sheet of paper on the table.

I picked it up and read:

"You *brute*! You will NEVER set eyes on my daughter AGAIN. As it
is you almost *killed* her last night with your REVOLTING *cruelty*! You
are WORSE, FAR WORSE, than the *Huns*! But GOD will punish you.
And *His* vengeance will not be long in coming."

XX

I looked at the clock.

If John were to catch his train he would have to leave in half an hour. One thing was certain. He must catch that train.

"You made enquiries?" I asked.

"Enquiries?" he laughed bitterly. "In the last six hours I've been everywhere—to police stations; railway stations; to all their old addresses."

"And you found?"

"Nothing. Not a trace. They packed up and left last night in a taxi, that's all I know. That was the only information I could wring out of the repulsive old landlady. I found Helga's note on the dressing-table of their bedroom. They have gone all right and it may take weeks to find them. And I—damn the war! I've half a mind to desert."

"And be court-martialled, and shot for a deserter? No. We will do better than that."

"You have got a plan. I can see it. Out with it, my dear old chap. It's a matter of life and death to Muriel and me." He wrung my hand almost hysterically in his excitement.

"I will find them," I said. "And when I have done so I will inform you immediately. Then by hook or by crook you must get leave and bring Muriel here. You, as her husband, are the only one who can do it. Here she will be safe. I don't think Helga would try any of her tricks here."

"Will you? My dear old chap, my dear old chap, I believe you will. I believe if anyone can do it you will. Thank God for a friend in need. If I hadn't you, my God! I don't know what I would do. The abominable old wretch! The hypocritical old—"

"Next time you will not inform her of your purpose," I interposed. "And now," as he commenced a new tirade, this time against his own folly, "you must be off. Stick to whacking the Germans until you hear from me. You are a Major now. What is the next step?"

John laughed. "No wonder hysterical old ladies consider you almost supernatural. Why, you've made me feel—almost hopeful."

XXI

Despite all my efforts, despite the reward of fifty pounds (which I afterwards increased to a hundred), three months passed before I discovered the whereabouts of John's wife.

I had thought it merely a matter of advertisement in a few daily papers. These proved futile. Even the offer of what must have appeared a most substantial reward elicited no information of any import. Wherever she was hiding, she must certainly have most loyal supporters.

It seemed almost inconceivable that in these enlightened days she and John's wife could have so utterly vanished. But apparently they had done so.

Scotland Yard could find no clue. No one had seen them go. No trace could be found of the taxi-driver who drove them. They had been seen at no railway station. They could by no possible means have left the country.

I called in a private firm of detectives. They too failed.

Then one morning a sudden idea came to me. In my young days amateur theatricals had been my hobby. And the following Saturday afternoon, donning suitable apparel, I went down to Bournemouth and presented myself as one looking for apartments to the landlady to whom John had applied the epithet "repulsive."

Certainly she was not beautiful. Fortunately I have had considerable experience of embittered and unbeautiful females, and of all the human race I have found them the most susceptible to flattery. No doubt owing to the fact that they meet so little of it.

At first Mrs Sommers eyed Mr Robinson, traveller in perfumery and toilet requisites, with the greatest suspicion. But the charms of Mr Robinson proving irresistible, he quickly found himself installed in an unsavoury bed-sitting-room on the first floor which he took for three months, cash in advance.

That evening Mr Peter Robinson dined with Mrs Sommers in the kitchen. Between them sundry bottles of stout, to the account of Mr Robinson, were consumed. Before the evening was out he was calling her Katie.

On Sunday evening Mr Robinson was forced to obey the inexorable call of duty. But promised to be back the Saturday following.

He was as good as his word.

This time he was received with open arms.

Towards the close of the evening, when the empty stout bottles were beginning to accumulate, Mr Robinson extracted a newspaper cutting from his pocket-book. "I'd like to get hold of this here hundred," he said.

"What hundred?" Katie's eyes sparkled.

Mr Robinson passed her the scrap of paper. Then slipped an arm around her ample waist. "Just do a fortnight in Town for the two of us, eh?"

Mrs Sommers frowned darkly at the paper.

Mr Robinson kissed her tenderly on the cheek. "It says they were last seen here," he said.

"Hush!" Mrs Sommers put a fat finger to her mouth. "It's a dead secret," she said. Then suspiciously: "You're not a detective, are you?"

"Do I look like a detective?" asked Mr Robinson scornfully. "You ought to know me better than that. What a suspicious little duck it is!" and he patted the hand nearest him.

"A fortnight in London for us two?" she whispered.

Mr Robinson, not without a qualm, perjured himself most passionately.

"They're 'ere," said Mrs Sommers.

Then, amid much merriment, in which the opening of bottles and the sound of kisses played due part, Mrs Sommers unfolded her story; which went, if memory does not deceive me, something like this:

"My, but she's a wonner! She says to me, says she, 'Mrs Sommers, when you want to disappear, just you stop where you are. It's the last place they'll ever think of lookin' for you.' So she packs up and they comes down 'ere to the kitchen, she leavin' a note that they've gone on the dressing-table. When the toff arrives, my word, but he is a swell, rollin' in money, she says, I tells him they drove off in a taxi. He carries on somethin' awful and insists on goin' into their rooms, which of course was empty, they bein' down 'ere in the kitchen all the time."

"Ha! ha! Hee! hee!" Mr Robinson laughed until the tears ran. "Ha! ha! Hee! hee! Did you ever hear the like? Ha! ha! Hee! hee!" He kissed Mrs Sommers twice very tenderly, and refilled her glass. "Now that's what I call a funny story. Ha! ha! Hee! hee! Down here all the time. Ha! ha! Hee! hee! You're a wonner, you are."

"And they're 'ere now."

"Not here?" Mr Robinson gasped incredulously.

"They are that. In their old rooms. Of course they don't go out, except her, and she only goes after dark. Would you like to see 'em?"

"No, no. What do I want to see them for?" hurriedly responded Mr Robinson. "This here is what I'm after. One hundred quid! And you might have had it all." He looked at her with unfeigned admiration. "Why in God's name didn't you have it?"

Mrs Sommers jerked her thumb towards the ceiling. "She's queer, pore thing," she said. "None of yer stuck-up toffs, but a real lidy for all. I can't say as how I likes all of her—she's—queer, but it's 'ard to refuse her anything."

"And didn't she give you anything to keep quiet and get rid of nosey Parkers?"

Mrs Sommers blushed. "No more'n you gave me to open me mouth."

"Well I never!" Mr Robinson was thunderstruck. Then, in a fit of generosity blurted out: "My dear, the hundred shall be yours."

Quite unexpectedly Mrs Sommers, who might have had the hundred for months past, burst into tears.

Men proverbially are deceivers, and proverbs contain at least a modicum of truth. Mrs Sommers, so far as I know, is even yet waiting for the perfidious Mr Robinson. And at times my own conscience is not quite clear; and that despite the fact that I sent her the hundred pounds in Bank of England notes.

XXII

Within a week John was with me. He was for going down to Bournemouth that very minute and removing Muriel from her mother, if necessary, by force. But I had a better plan, in which Mr Robinson would be called upon to play his last part. For I had grave doubts as to John being able to get into the house at all, so long as the faithful Mrs Sommers was on guard. Had she not foiled Scotland Yard and all my detectives?

Forthwith the following telegram was despatched:

> Meet me Charing Cross Station under the clock seven p.m. to-morrow cheerio.—PETER.

John was sceptical. "How do you know she will be there?" he asked. "She can scarcely leave at such short notice."

"Put yourself in her place. Conceive, if you can, her solitary life of drab drudgery, without ambition, without objective, without hope, without love. Then introduce Romance, if only in the shape of a Mr Robinson. And wouldn't you follow it to the ends of the earth, let alone to Charing Cross?"

"It would depend upon Romance's appearance," laughed John.

"Not if you were a woman. It is the spirit of the thing a woman is always seeking. To her the form is merely incidental. She will be there. Not a doubt of it. I am told Mr Robinson can be quite attractive."

The following afternoon John and I motored to Bournemouth and presented ourselves at the apartment house of Mrs Kate Sommers. A young girl opened the door.

"Was Mrs Sommers in?"

"No, Mrs Sommers was not in. She had been called to London on important business."

We expressed sorrow, and I was just explaining that we had come to see the invalid lady upstairs, when a door to our left opened stealthily and a face appeared.

"It's Helga!" cried John, and dashed in.

Explaining to the girl that the gentleman was the young lady's husband, and that he had just come home from the war and was very anxious to see her, I shut the front door and followed John into the room.

When I arrived he had Helga Stourcross fast in his arms and she was struggling and kicking and beating him about the face with clenched fists.

"You shan't have her! You shan't have her!" she was shrieking. Before the fire sat Muriel, quite unmoved.

"Stop that!" I said, "or I will send for the police."

That stopped her. John loosed his hold and went to Muriel.

I faced Helga, deathly pale now. "The game is up," I said.

"He shan't have her," she began again.

"He is her husband, and has every right, by law, to take her. We have a motor at the door and she is coming with us now."

Again I saw the wicked light blaze up in her eyes. Then it died down and a look of cunning crept into them.

"Very well," she said. "I presume I may go upstairs and pack her things?"

"Yes, if I go with you," I replied.

Together we left the room. Outside was the girl who had let us in. Helga gave her a look of positive loathing. "You shall pay for this," she hissed. "Mrs Sommers will half kill you when she gets back."

"Oh! Oh! Oh!" The girl commenced to sob. "Oh! Oh! Oh!" Her sobbing followed us up the stairs. The poor child seemed literally terrified, but there was no time to more than pat her head and bid her not to take any notice. Everything was all right.

Upstairs in the bedroom Helga turned to me. "Why are you so cruel?" she cried. "Why do you persecute me in this way? Haven't you a spark of pity for a poor mother?"

"Pack, please," I ordered curtly.

With that she commenced to pull out boxes and rummage in drawers and cupboards. Never have I seen such confusion, which is a sure sign of a disorderly mind, except among the lowest strata of society. And all the while she kept muttering to herself, like one possessed, threats, oaths, the most hideous blasphemies.

The packing seemed an interminable task, and time was passing.

"You had better send these things on to my address," I said. "Meanwhile we will put a few things into this bag."

"That's mine," she snapped.

"This will do." I indicated a dressing-case with M.T. on it.

Reluctantly she stuffed in a nightdress, brush and comb, slippers, and sundry odds and ends.

"Now a coat," I said, fastening the case, "and a travelling rug."

Those she handed to me.

Thus equipped I went downstairs.

I knocked at the sitting-room door. John was on his knees. His wife had not moved. She might have been deaf and dumb, blind, paralysed, dead, so still she was, so void of expression her face, eyes open, staring sightless into space.

"Come along," I called. "Carry her."

And while he carried her into the car, I waited at the door for fear of any further interference on the part of Helga Stourcross.

She did not reappear. I only saw her when, safely ensconced in the car, we were driving away. She was leaning out of an upper window; and never shall I forget the satanic look on her face. I was thankful the others had not seen it.

XXIII

When one's life-work lies almost exclusively among the sick, one is in grave danger of coming to regard human suffering as a necessary evil. More and more is one tempted to rely upon nostrums or the knife. It is so easy to come to consider that truly marvellous combination of spiritual and material elements, the human being, as a mere machine, to be treated mechanically.

And yet this is scarcely the way of wisdom. For a sick body is but the symptom of a sick soul. And it is the soul, not the symptom, that requires treatment.

"Rise, take up thy bed, and walk," was the order of our Wisest Physician; followed later by the injunction: "Behold, thou art made whole: sin no more, lest a worse thing come unto thee." Not: You must be operated upon immediately. Or: Take these pills three times a day.

A miracle?

Yes; a miracle of wisdom; love-taught, not learned in any school.

For twenty centuries the world has had a prescription that has never been known to fail, a veritable panacea for all its complaints, so childishly simple as to seem not worth the trial: "Love one another." But we have preferred mysterious formulas, clever operations, and pills.

And never was the world more sick. And never were there more physicians.

Blow expense, we say, as we set about building our new little earths. In schools, schools, and more schools, we see salvation. We build more churches, when those already built are almost empty. Our governments grow more and more expensive. We are surfeited with brains, whose brilliance blinds us to all common sense. Never were more brilliant politicians, more brilliant preachers, more brilliant teachers, more brilliant scientists, inventors, physicians, and surgeons. And never was more unhappiness.

With microscopes we seek the Elixir of Life in strange places; nor think to find it at home in our own hearts. We have divorced Science from his spiritual bride, and have married him to Materialism, that past-mistress of deception.

And Love, the mainspring of the universe, the power behind all creation, the motive of all creation, the seat and source of all inspiration, all healing, all happiness, has come to mean to this enlightened age mere sexual pleasure.

Like children intoxicated with their first freedom, we have dethroned our fathers' God, dragged Him boisterously through the mire of our city streets, and with foolish laughter dropped Him at the feet of a painted prostitute. Then, later, wept. Now wonder, sadly, why the world's all wrong.

Despite Mrs Travers' most pitiable condition, I had no qualms as I felt her icy hand and the pulse that was scarcely perceptible. For Love was here. Not in me. I in this was nothing. To me it was given to watch only, and pray.

I watched and prayed.

John's face was transfigured; the light in his eyes was of no earthly origin; and the words that fell softly from his lips as he called his beloved from the dark shadows wherein she wandered were liquid music that yet lingers in my heart.

And his beloved came back. Not with the horrified start of the sleep-walker suddenly awakened. But as a happy child awakes—a soft flush stealing first across the face; a little trembling of the lips as trees tremble at the dawn; a little fluttering of the eyelids as flutter waking birds; and then the smile of recognition and new life.

So Muriel returned to John.

It was the beginning of new life where all was beauty, a new honeymoon. Never have I seen human beings so happy. No thing of matter was that love of theirs. Had it not worked a miracle? It was as though a flame from Heaven itself had fused them, soul, mind, body, into one.

My old bachelor house was transformed, as by a magic wand, into Love's sanctuary; to which one came humbly; and went away refreshed.

My old butler, the housekeeper, the maids, each and all were affected. The bondage of years seemed to fall away from them. The old stern service gave place to service with smiles.

That fortnight was very pleasant.

Then Duty called. John donned again his fighting kit. And half our light was gone.

But Muriel remained.

Muriel. I see her now very frequently, for she has endeared herself to me as no woman has ever done—except my mother. In her widow's weeds she makes a picture of which one never tires. The sun-streaked hair; the wistful eyes that seem always to be looking through and beyond one as though at some distant vision; the mouth so mobile that all the heart's emotions are seen there; the brow serene as the brain behind it; the cheeks to which the colour softly comes as Memory dips her brush in some past loveliness, and as softly goes.

Were I a marrying man, were I younger, more worthy, I might be emboldened to rise up from her feet and offer her my hand—such as it is. At times I have been sorely tempted. But she is not one to be satisfied with substitutes. For she has known Reality, which is Love; and spells it JOHN.

To her John is not dead, but promoted, for noble services rendered, to some happier and more lovely place; to which she, if so be she, too, renders noble service, will in God's good time be promoted.

Thus I am content to watch her rendering her noble services as a nurse in an Infant Welfare Home. And if sometimes I can give her some little pleasure, am able sometimes to render her some little service, it is with the sure knowledge that she is John's, as surely as though he were walking by her side in the flesh. That knowledge is our seal of friendship.

So she remains and will remain until the end of the chapter my Lady of the Lamp; for she has shown me Love, such as I never hoped to see. High aloft she holds the light, revealing to all within its radius the path to Perfection and making clear the pitfalls at their feet. And I thank God that I, too, have come within its compass.

No wonder John loved her, nay, must love her still.

No wonder she loves John. For it was his touch that awakened her; his love that fertilised hers and made it to bear such rich, rich fruit; and his death, or the deed that caused his death, that set her free.

Substitutes for such as she?

XXIV

Muriel never discussed her mother. It was a banned subject between us. When first I had mentioned Mrs Stourcross with the object of finding out something more about that remarkable woman, a look of positive terror had crept into her eyes. "Don't let's talk about her," she said. "She spoils things so."

Thus it was settled. Never again did I mention her mother's name in Muriel's presence. But I could not forget the woman. Thoughts of her returned persistently to my mind. And the memory of that malignant face staring from the window was not easily put away. Furthermore, I felt sure that we had not yet seen the last of her.

Although I did not believe that she would try any of her tricks in my house, nevertheless, I took every possible precaution. The staff had their instructions and such information as I considered necessary. To enter the house she would have to emulate the "cat burglar." And to guard against any contingency outside, Muriel, at my urgent request, never went out unattended.

Several months passed in complete tranquillity. John, who had again distinguished himself and been awarded the D.S.O., had come and gone like a knight of old.

What rejoicings when he arrived! What stir and flutter! What excitement both down and upstairs! For were we not living Romance? And is not Romance as dear to ourselves as to cook and kitchen-maid?

And Muriel. What fairer ladye could brave knight wish for? One could scarcely credit that she had once been so pale and lifeless.

What wonders Love had worked for her, for him, for us all! At its faery touch the house itself had become a castle, theirs; and we their most loving retainers and willing servitors.

Then forth the brave knight had gone again to do battle for a finer cause than that of Chivalry. Fair hands, if they did not gird on his armour, at any rate straightened his "Sam Brown." His buttons, if not his shield, shone like the sun. And the kitchen-maid wept for us, too old, too civilised, perhaps, to weep.

It was about a month after John's last leave—unconsciously we had formed the habit of dating events from those flying visits of his— that a whole series of minor accidents began to happen; of themselves insignificant, but in the light of future events decidedly ominous.

I was the first to suffer.

While getting out of bed one morning I slipped and sprained an ankle. No sooner had I recovered from this than I was knocked down one night by a motor-lorry immediately outside my own door. Fortunately, I was thrown clear and escaped with a scalp wound and a few bruises. Next my dog, Toby, a wire-haired fox-terrier and a great favourite, in the prime of life, expired suddenly of an undiagnosable disease. Poison was out of the question. Then my housekeeper caught influenza, which turned to septic pneumonia. We had a hard fight to pull her round. Without doubt it was Muriel who saved her life.

No sooner was she out of danger than my cook, who had been with me for years, left; suffering as I then thought with delusions, induced as I suspected by drink, for she insisted that the house was haunted. There was no question but that she was most thoroughly scared, though by what I could never elucidate.

The cook's fears spread to the kitchen-maid, who begged permission to go to work in a munition factory. This I could not conscientiously refuse her.

The parlour-maid, too, was affected. But stayed on in deference to the wishes of her young man, who was in the Coldstreams, and invariably spent his leave with us.

McKenzie, who had grown old in my service, also began to become troublesome. He would act in the most irritating and irrational way; nosing furtively about the place, looking fearfully behind him, and speaking in hoarse whispers. All my efforts to cajole him into a peaceful frame of mind proved fruitless: and at my satire he would merely shake his grizzled head and look pityingly upon me. We were "overlooked," that was all I could get out of him. Apparently he had met the phenomenon before in his native Highlands. And no arguments of mine would convince him to the contrary.

Muriel alone remained unaffected. What we should have done without her during this trying time I do not know. As the staff dropped out, she took on more and more of the work, despite all my objections. And the efficient manner in which she carried out her self-imposed duties was truly remarkable in one of her upbringing. She was unflagging in her efforts and determined that the house should run as it did before. But for her I should have lost McKenzie, of that I am convinced.

It seemed with her to be a matter of honour. It was almost as though she were inspired. Looking back now I think, although she never mentioned her suspicions to me, that she suspected the cause of our troubles and slaved thus to counteract it.

One thing she proved to me: that Labour strikes will never accomplish the end of England so long as there are Muriels among our educated women.

But work as she would, our troubles were not at an end. As a fitting climax, I fell down the front steps one morning and fractured the right femur in two places, both compound fractures.

I might well have broken my neck, for I fell most violently. It was almost as though some one had given me a tremendous push from behind.

When I came to my senses, McKenzie, muttering darkly, had me in his arms.

By this time we were the centre of a small crowd, and by all that was extraordinary, the first person upon whom I opened my eyes was Helga Stourcross; with a smile upon her face which I can only describe as devilish.

As she caught my eye she edged away into the crowd.

This accident tied me to my bed for several weeks. At first I had thought it best to go to Hospital, for Muriel had work enough in all conscience without my adding to it. But upon consideration I decided that, incapacitated though I was, my presence would afford her some measure of protection. She was in danger, not a doubt of it. Not for nothing was Helga Stourcross in London. Not for nothing had she been there outside the house.

I even began to suspect her of being in some way responsible for our recent misfortunes.

The thing was absurd, of course. On a par with McKenzie's "overlooking," and the "Evil Eye" of the Irish peasantry. A hark back to the Dark Ages.

And yet, in spite of Common Sense and Reason, the idea persisted.

Lying in bed, I attempted to thrust out this most stupid superstition. But it would not be pushed out. Like some monstrous bird of ill-omen Helga Stourcross brooded over my bed.

I had McKenzie bring me up from the library an old book on Witchcraft. Remarkable how the idea had persisted through the ages among all sorts and conditions of people. This belief in the Powers of Darkness was as ancient and, it would seem, as well authenticated as the belief in the Powers of Light.

God and Devil, Good and Evil, Light and Darkness; were not these but names for those great psychic influences, Love and Hate? That dragged the soul, as the sea is dragged by the moon, now this way and now that, to splendid heights, and to the most miserable depths. That kept the soul astir, always moving, and so never stagnant.

If Love had his "miracles"—and had I not seen them?—why not Hate have his? If by thinking Love to a third person one could do him good, why not do harm by thinking Hate? Had I not years ago accepted this in theory, and did I not practise it as Coué was doing in Paris?

Had I not laughed at the report of the subcommittee appointed by the Medical Council in 1909 to investigate "Spiritual Healing," and pointed out that not once in all their learned discussions was the word Love mentioned? Had I not likened them to babes in the wood, unable to see, and so unwilling to admit the sun; and arguing, most brilliantly, about the light: what it was, and whence it came?

If Love had his miracles, why not Hate?

And then the picture crossed my mind of Muriel lying there upon her bed, so stricken and so still as to seem almost dead: beyond all power of medicine. Yet John woke her. And her words, which I had thought too ridiculous for a moment's consideration, came back to me. "You don't believe in witches, Doctor Toogood? I can show you one—my mother. *She can make things happen. She has power, tremendous, awful power. She can kill*"— And Helga's face rose up before my eyes, smiling satanically.

Ridiculous nonsense, said Common Sense. You are ill, man, overwrought; and can't think straight. The woman is becoming an obsession. Put the thing away; and try a novel.

*

I tried a novel; and put that away. Obsession or no obsession, ill or no, Helga vexed me enormously. She seemed to be in the room with me: cruel, cunning, hating horribly.

Here was one who could hate. Here was one whom I could picture hating steadily, for hours on end; hating unflinchingly to one purpose: her own ends. Here was one who had learned to focus her thoughts into one channel and keep them there; that channel always some one's harm.

Here was no paltry pleasure lover: no puny, shrunken soul; but a woman, elemental, big of heart and brain, big of soul; too big to wear the little bonds of Civilisation.

Here was a woman who could love, who would stake all for love; and having lost it, would hate, unfeignedly, without fear or hope of favour. A genius, who had missed the road to God; and so struck out at everything that seemed to hold her back; at God Himself, because she had missed His way.

Here was a Witch—You don't believe in witches, Doctor Toogood?—who might have been a goddess. Who would not fear to call up Satan; an she could. Who would harness twenty Devils to her chariot; an she could see Love's face again.

XXV

A few days after I was carried to bed I received a letter from John. "It seems ridiculous," he wrote, "but I am anxious about you good people. I keep thinking that you are in some tremendous danger. It must be subconscious, for I haven't much time for thinking outside this show. It may be due to the newspaper reports of Zepp raids and so forth.

"By the way, have you heard anything of Helga? I keep thinking of her, too. Although it is difficult to imagine what harm she could do now. For I know, my dear old chap, that you always keep your eyes open.

"Last week I received a parcel from the Army and Navy Stores. It contained, you will never guess, a steel breastplate! Who could have sent it, I can't imagine. It certainly wasn't Muriel. She is far too sensible to saddle a man with useless encumbrances. The only clue was a slip of paper on which was printed: TO WARD OFF THE SHELLS.

"Its arrival, as you can imagine, created quite a sensation, for I opened it in the Mess, and such things are to us an abomination. We, whatever the Germans may do, don't go about in armour-plate while our men go naked.

"I gave the beastly thing to my batman, who wears it, I believe; for recently his chest has increased enormously. Rather heroic of him! For it weighs like the devil."

Ten days later I received a short note:—

"My batman was killed yesterday. Poor beggar! A sniper took him in the gullet, just above that infernal breastplate."

That was the last word either Muriel or I had from him, our next news being a telegram from the War Office announcing the fact that he was dangerously wounded.

Muriel received the news magnificently. As though armed with some intimate knowledge, she refused to be fearful. "He will get better," she said. "I know he will get better."

After a short interval we heard that he was being retained with No. 1 Field Ambulance until the D.D.M.S. thought it advisable to move him. "We will keep him here, my dear Mrs Travers," wrote that gentleman, "until he is out of danger or until the Germans make it too hot for us here. Meanwhile he is getting on very nicely and sends all sorts of messages to you. He has quite made up his mind that he is going to pull round, which is half the battle.

"One thing more. I am to tell you on no account to attempt to come out here, but to stay where you are. On this point your good man is very emphatic. And I am inclined to agree with him that any form of excitement, other than what we are now undergoing, would not be good for him."

This latter injunction Muriel obeyed to the letter. Indeed, her time was so fully occupied that she scarcely left the house, doing most of her shopping by telephone.

And then one morning she disappeared.

I had missed her morning ministrations, but put it down to some fresh domestic difficulty. The appearance of McKenzie as he brought me my lunch caused me some apprehension.

To extract information from McKenzie is never an easy matter. The Spanish Inquisition in its palmiest days would have found him a most difficult subject. This paucity of words is, if anything, an asset in his professional capacity and adds, if such were possible, to the dignity of his bearing. At times like these one found it trying.

My enquiries as to Mrs Travers' whereabouts met with a shake of the head.

"Out or in?" I asked.

Another shake of the head.

"For God's sake speak up, man. Out with it."

The dejection in his face became even more dreadful. "Missis—Travers—has—gone, sirrr," he announced slowly, solemnly, as if coining appropriate words. Then as suddenly as though a tap had been turned on somewhere inside him, his native tongue triumphed and a veritable flood of speech followed, in the vernacular of his native village. Only emotion long pent up could have accounted for such an unheard-of outburst.

From it all I elicited that a note had arrived by special messenger, and upon reading it Muriel had at once put on her hat and gone out, telling McKenzie that she would be back very shortly. That had been at ten o'clock. It was now half-past one. Without a doubt we were "overlooked."

McKenzie groaned encouragingly.

Tied as I was, there was nothing to do but await events. Instructing McKenzie to inform me the moment Mrs Travers returned, I dismissed him, for his gloom was infectious.

Try as I would, I could not feel easy in my mind. So many misfortunes had happened to us that it was difficult not to anticipate them. What could have happened? Some accident? Had she been knocked down, run over, killed? A hundred-and-one dreadful possibilities flashed through my mind. And the note? Who had sent that? Had Helga anything to do with it?

Then I commenced to laugh at the recollection of McKenzie's face and at my own ridiculous fears. Of course, the note was from

John. He had been evacuated from France and had just landed up at some London Hospital, and had, naturally enough, taken the first possible opportunity of informing Muriel. And Muriel had at once put on her hat and gone to him. They would be together now. What more natural?

Most resolutely I attempted to keep my thoughts upon this happy picture. I recalled to mind their wonderful love for one another. I tried to recapture the glamour of those days when they had been together under this same roof and together had made of it a place of enchantment. Again and again I reassured myself that Love must conquer. That it was stronger than Death. That no waters could drown it.

But always a face would intrude: the face of Helga Stourcross, as I had last seen it outside my own front door. And it leered at me in triumph.

Evening came, and still no news.

Had Muriel gone to John, they would most certainly have understood my anxiety and sent me some message. I became convinced that all my worst fears would be confirmed. By some means or other Helga Stourcross had got her daughter back.

But how?

The note received by Muriel that morning seemed to be the key to the situation. Supposing it to have been from her mother, what had it contained to make her walk out without a word? And granted that it had contained a message urgent enough to make her walk out without a word, what was keeping her? Did Helga still retain some hypnotic influence over her? I doubted it. For Muriel had developed a strength of character remarkable in so young a woman and a sense of duty rare in any woman. Only a matter of urgent duty would have called her away, I felt certain. And Muriel, as she now was, detained against her will, would be a match for most women.

A match for Helga? Had she not been but a few months since as clay in Helga's hands? Had not John been as clay in Helga's hands? And I, myself, had I not felt her power? The woman was strong and vindictive, and would stick at nothing to accomplish her ends.

What were her ends? What was her motive?

Was it Love, in its crudest, blindest, most possessive form; love worked and twisted into insensate jealousy? Was it Hate, generated by opposition to her will? Or was it merely a matter of Money?

Love, Hate, Money. One of these three, or a combination of these three, was the motive power of most human action. To one or other, or combination of one or other, could be attributed most human weal and woe.

"And the greatest of these is Love."

Quite without context the sentence thrust itself into my thoughts. Was Love the greatest? Certainly I had always believed it to be so; and always had found it so. If one accepted that hypothesis, why worry that I was tied to my bed and incapable of any action in this crisis in the affairs of my friends? Love would triumph. And these two had Love; a love, selfless, perfect, such as I had never met before. Why not leave it at that, and rest content?

That night for all my mental tribulation and the pain in my leg I slept very soundly.

But it is not in human nature to rest content for long. As men we do not possess, nor are we, I think, expected to possess, the blind faith of children. Else ambition, with all its character-forming qualities, would end. Would end all struggle and strife and war, all soul-stirrings, all heart-shakings. Would end all action, initiative, resource, and all progress; all motive for selflessness and self-sacrifice and splendid, or ignoble, deeds. Evolution itself would end. And the human race would die of inaction and over-indulgence, or degenerate into a fellowship of fat, sleek, unctuous beings, not individuals; equal in all things, quite inhuman, and altogether ungodly.

The following morning, as there was no news of any kind, I bestirred myself over the telephone, and in the course of the day discovered that John had been removed to a hospital in Rouen, but was likely to be evacuated in the course of a few days as he was making excellent progress. Haemoptysis had ceased, and the gunshot wound in his chest was healing satisfactorily.

All of which was excellent news. Forthwith I decided not to break to him the news of Muriel's disappearance. It would only retard his recovery, and who knew whether she might not have returned before ever he landed in England.

I also arranged for an advertisement to be inserted in the Personal Columns of half a dozen morning papers, and had a lengthy interview with the head of a leading firm of private detectives.

But I might have saved myself this trouble. For by the last delivery I received the following from an address in Clapham:

MY DEAR DOCTOR TOOGOOD,

This is to thank you for your kindness to my darling child. I am *delighted* to see her looking so *very* much better. London always suited her. She is with me now as she *feels* that she *owes* a DUTY to her poor mother, and has not the heart to let me die among strangers.

I am very ill—dying, I think. I fear it is cancer of the throat. The pain is terrible. I shall not be in *your way* for long.

In the circumstances I know that you will not mind her leaving you so unexpectedly, nor will John. Why not come over and see us? But of course you can't. What an unfortunate accident! I trust you are making satisfactory progress.

Yours very sincerely.

Here was scrawled a signature, almost unintelligible, but which might have been deciphered as "Helga Stourcross." The rest of the letter was written in the copperplate of a child.

A laconic postscript followed:

"I am here of my own free will."

This was signed in the same childish copperplate: "Muriel Stourcross."

At least a dozen times I read and re-read that remarkable communication, and each fresh reading brought fresh interpretation.

On the face of it, it was almost natural. What more natural than that Muriel in response to an urgent summons should have hurried off to her dying mother? Who could resist such an appeal? What more natural than that the dying mother should have sent for her daughter? That Helga, about to die and in need of forgiveness, should herself be willing to forgive?

On the face of it the letter was what one might have expected under the circumstances. And yet the more I read it, the more I found myself doubting, cynical; distrusting and hating very heartily this dying woman.

Was she actually dying? Or even ill? Might not this be an extraordinary audacious plan to get her daughter back? No dying woman could have signed her name more illegibly. Could any educated person, however much *in extremis*, have done it worse? Was it not overdone?

Then the postscript; what did that conceal? Why was it signed Muriel Stourcross and not Muriel Travers? And that absurd copperplate, so childish, so unlike Muriel's own handwriting, who had written it? If Muriel had written it, it implied a forgetting, a slipping back upon the Sands of Time. If she had written it, beyond a doubt it meant that she had come again under her mother's hypnotic influence and that her identity had once more become hidden behind the veil of her mother's weaving.

My conclusions made me acutely uneasy. Helga seemed to be winning all along the line. John, myself, all her enemies were out of action. Nothing could be done but await events and trust the Providence that orders the wheels of Fate.

XXVI

Whether from anxiety or whatever cause, my recovery was by no means as rapid as it should have been, and before ever I was able to do more than hobble about my bedroom on crutches John had been transferred to a London hospital.

His arrival meant complications. For now he would most certainly have to be told the tragic news. Up to then I had felt it to be my duty to keep him in the dark, as a sudden shock might well have had fatal results. My letters to him, I must confess, had teemed with misstatements and fictitious explanations. One and all contained not only very sound reasons why Muriel had not written, but loving messages from the lady herself. For I had judged that Helga would never have written to him or allowed her daughter to write; and his letters to me indicated as much.

Needless to say I had kept myself informed as to Helga's movements, and had quickly learnt that, not only was she not dying, but that she appeared to be enjoying the best of health. On the contrary, it was Muriel who was very ill, according to my information. They were still in apartments at Clapham.

The day after John's arrival came a telephone message for Muriel to come over immediately. I replied, making an appointment for the following day.

With considerable difficulty and the aid of McKenzie I managed to navigate the stairs, get into the motor, and arrive at John's bedside.

Poor fellow; he had had a bad time of it. The bullet had penetrated the left chest, breaking a couple of ribs, and perforating the lung tissues, where it still remained embedded and was likely to remain so, as an operation was, of course, out of the question. It had missed the heart by half an inch. Haemoptysis and septicæmia had been the gravest dangers. But he was out of the wood now, and delighted to see me. Where was Muriel?

The inevitable question had to be answered. Looking him in the face I could not lie. As gently as I could I broke the news to him.

The effect was terrible.

"What, gone? Gone? Gone again," he kept repeating in a husky whisper. "Gone? All gone? Oh, my God! Oh, my God!"

The haggard, twitching face, the eyes, tearless, dilated, grown terrible, were more than I could bear. This was my brother, my dear, dear brother; and I had hurt him so. I wanted to take him in my arms, to kiss and comfort him as I had often done in childhood. But we were men. And I must either run away or look down upon his agony.

I could not run away, and so looked down with vision blurred. Nor could I speak, stammered only: "All right soon. Soon get her back. Everything all right soon."

At that he laughed. And that was worse.

Then on a sudden he sat up, eyes starting, arms waving as though to ward off some enemy. "Those dreams! Those damnable, devilish dreams! Oh, my God! Oh, my God!"

He sank back exhausted, groaning: "Oh, my God!"

Presently he fell asleep. And I was thankful enough to hobble away on McKenzie's arm.

At the end of the week I visited John again. The improvement in him was remarkable. "I'll be up out of this very soon, my dear old chap," he said as he shook my hand. "I've been scrimshanking too long, and there is work to do."

There was a quiet determination in his voice and in his eyes a quiet courage.

"Now tell me everything," he said, "from the beginning, please. I'll not make an ass of myself again."

When I had done so, he again shook my hand. "My dear old chap," he said, "what a time you must have had! I bet you've blessed the day you gave us house-room and took upon yourself our troubles. My dear old chap, to blame yourself when you have been the best friend that ever a man had. What more could you do?"

"I might have—" I began.

John laughed heartily. "I don't forget that you once became Mr Peter Robinson for us. When a man of your standing does that I think he has gone his limit. And the perjury you've been practising these past weeks, what price that? And the prickings of your dear old conscience. By the Lord Harry, you deserve the V.C."

That was John all over, always generous, always forgetting his own for other people's troubles. A mixture of Bayard and Quixote, lovable always.

And then we made our plans. We would leave matters as they were until John was up and about. There would be no attempt to communicate with Muriel, but observation would be kept upon them. Then what we had done before we would do again. We would remove Muriel from her mother. But this time she and John would go to that dream-cottage of theirs somewhere in Cornwall.

"And Heaven help her if she interferes with us again," said John.

I was to remember his words.

XXVII

A fortnight later Helga, Muriel, and an elderly woman left Clapham and took the night train to Liverpool. The private detective whom I had engaged, a most astute fellow although quite uneducated, was on the same train and sent me a wire from the first stopping-place to that effect. It reached me next morning.

My first idea was to telephone at once to John. But upon reflection I decided not to do so, as it would be impossible for him to do anything. Moreover, it would be almost impossible for them to leave the country with the restrictions then in force, and in any case the detective had his instructions not to lose sight of them. I decided therefore to await events.

Further news was soon forthcoming. At Liverpool they had gone to a small temperance hotel, where they had booked rooms in the names of Mrs Reginald Tower, Miss Tower, and maid. Miss Tower and the maid never left their room while Mrs Reginald Tower was haunting the shipping offices. "They are hoping to make a getaway," wrote the detective. "But I'll be there."

Four days later I heard that they had gone to the Isle of Man. From Douglas, which appeared to be the capital and principal seaport, quite unknown to me but from the works of Hall Caine, I received another letter. They had arrived safely and were in rooms at one of the innumerable boarding establishments, "Monaville." The place was deserted. And as for the war, the inhabitants did not seem to know that there was one. "Plenty of everything and no restrictions. A blooming Paradise," wrote my informant. "The beau-ideal for a rest-cure. Madame imagines herself as safe as houses and goes out as large as life. We're the best of pals. I'm a wounded hero and will continue such until further instructions!"

A further letter informed me that they had taken a furnished house in a little seaside place called Port St Mary's, which was labelled "a dead and alive hole."

Still another read: "They seem to have settled down here for life. Madame is no end of a swell, entertaining all the toffs, and they don't half make a fuss of her. Yesterday she called on the Governor. She is still Mrs Reginald Tower. I must say she has a nerve.

"The girl, I beg pardon, Mrs Travers, is said to be consumptive and not quite all there, due to shock caused by the death of her young man, a Captain in the Coldstream Guards, who was killed in action during the retreat from Mons. My oath, but she has a nerve.

"P.S.—I have got the job as chauffeur. The old girl has just bought herself a swanky car—a saloon—and has taken no end of a tumble to me."

Upon receipt of this, and out of curiosity, I looked up the Army Lists from 1914. And surely enough the name Captain Reginald Tower did appear as serving in the Coldstream Guards. Helga was certainly astute. But Mr Albert Edward Brown was still more astute. And his letters acted as a veritable tonic to John, and were warranted to dissipate his deepest depression.

XXVIII

"The problem is how to do it without making a frightful scene," said John.

For perhaps the twentieth time we were discussing ways and means to circumvent Helga, and we seemed no nearer to a solution.

"I hate scenes," he continued. "And after all, she is Muriel's mother, and one can't wash one's dirty linen in public."

"That excludes the Law Courts," I said.

"Quite."

"Well, then, if I were you I should go over to the Isle of Man and see the Lieutenant-Governor," I suggested. "I have looked him up and I feel sure we have mutual friends. He is an Anglo-Indian, too, and without doubt will know your people. Put the matter to him plainly and give him your proofs."

"I wish you could come along," John said. "But of course you can't. Somehow I've got the wind up. A woman has got such a pull and one can't hammer her. Then again, I've developed such a beast of a temper."

I laughed.

"Oh, I know you think that I've the temper of a saint. I used to be a philosophical kind of a beggar, slow to anger and all that sort of thing. But now I can't be certain of keeping a hold on myself. I've seen red too often in France. I see it now—sometimes— when I think of Helga. My dear old chap, I would love—actually love—to kill that old she-devil; take her neck in my hands and twist it like this."

He made a horrid contortion with his hands, and I saw that his face had grown deathly pale.

"You have been brooding too long on your troubles. You are not yourself. Try looking on the bright side. Cultivate an optimistic outlook on life."

Something in his face had frightened me, and I found myself voicing the fatuous sentiments all we doctors come to use; sentiments so easy to express, so difficult to attain.

John looked at me and laughed. "How frightened we civilised people are of the primitive, aren't we? We've eliminated a lot of things in our nature; we hide a lot more. Most wonderfully we have learnt to control our feelings and mask our emotions. All very excellent and as it should be. Until something—prolonged strain or ill-health—undermines our self-control. Then our conventional coverings drop off; the masks drop off; and we stand up naked savages, with battle-scarred bodies, and faces streaked with passion. You were never in a bayonet charge, were you?"

I confessed that I had not had that pleasure.

John laughed again. "But you were Peter Robinson," he said. "And I should call Peter Robinson a distinctly primitive person. Didn't he drink stout and—er—embrace the cook or something?

"Somewhat younger and with careful drilling," he continued, "I can see him a perfectly good soldier, bayoneting Boches to beat the band, as our American friends would put it."

"Conceivably possible," I replied, "provided the necessity was great enough."

"Exactly," said John. "In the present case we have an enormous necessity. And here, remember, we are dealing with such primitive emotions as Love and Hate. I know now, being naked and unashamed, in my own eyes at any rate, that I do love and I do hate enormously, as much, if not more than our forefathers who ran about with clubs. I also know that at times of intense excitement I have found myself controlled by and not controlling my emotions. That is why I am afraid.

"Of course, it has got to be done," he continued. "I only want to let you know that I don't like the job. Anyway, I think I will take your advice and try the Lieutenant-Governor. I am leaving here in a day or two, so if you can pull any strings, my dear old chap, pull 'em like blazes."

So much had John's fears impressed me, opening up as they did possibilities that had never even crossed my mind, that I determined, come what might, to accompany him to the Isle of Man. So small are our minds that we can perceive only one trouble at a time, and at this time John's troubles to me were of such paramount importance that the world war had almost lost its significance.

Arrangements were made for my leaving at the end of the week. I had obtained an introduction to the Lieutenant-Governor of the Isle of Man from a person of considerable influence at the Foreign Office. I had even instructed the detective to be prepared for our arrival, when a letter arrived from John. It was dated the previous day and posted in Liverpool. It read:

MY DEAR OLD CHAP,

I made up my mind last night, and here I am. To-morrow I cross to the Isle of Man, a four or five hours' trip. There are one or two German submarines knocking about, they tell me, but they are not interfering with the Isle of Man boats as there is a large German prisoners' camp there. So to-morrow, please God, I shall see Muriel.

To think that to-morrow, after all these days and weeks, I shall actually see her, hear her, touch her, inhale the fragrance of her, feel her breath upon my cheek, is an intoxication of the senses, of the very soul, quite incomprehensible to so sober a citizen as yourself.

Never having loved, you cannot know my feelings. Have you ever had an ambition? Worked, sweated, slaved day after day, week after week, year after year? And at last seen its conclusion in sight? If so, you have experienced but one-thousandth part of what I now experience.

We men laugh at Love—until it comes to us, tears the very soul from our bodies, and sweeps it on golden pinions to the gates of Paradise. Then our laughter dies away. Tears overflow the heart and mist the sight. Our self is overpowered; made nothing; melts away into a delirium of sheer delight.

To-morrow! One sunset more; one sunrise. And then the great day is begun. A day that knows no time, no season, but stretches on unto Eternity. Now I walk on air. To-morrow I will fly on golden pinions.

I am drunk—put it down at that—drunk with dreams of Love.

John's sudden departure, alone, caused me considerable misgivings. But his letter consoled me. Not once had he mentioned Helga. Not a thought of hate was in it. It was a love-letter, written from the very soul of him: a letter such as men seldom write to men. But John was different. There had always seemed to be a bond between us, an invisible cord that bound us closer than brothers.

I read the letter over again. "Never having loved." He was wrong there. I had loved his mother and mine, an old-fashioned sort of love, perhaps; with more of calm about it, and a certain reverence. I loved him, too, as one might love a younger brother, with a protective, almost paternal instinct. I was sorry, more sorry than I could say, that I had allowed him to go alone. If anything happened to him I should be terribly upset.

But this Love of his was altogether of another order, infinitely bigger than himself. Something stupendous. A mystery revealed only to the very few. A precious gift from God, entrusted only to those who could appreciate it. The poet Shelley had it. I turned to his works, and opened the volume at random. There upon the first page, almost at my finger-point, I read:

> "Thou art the wine whose drunkenness is all that we can desire, O Love."

"I am drunk with dreams of Love." John's words.

Was it a conscious or unconscious plagiarism? It certainly seemed like it. I put the thought aside. It was too small, I felt, for the occasion. One might dissect a man's body and be justified. But one could not stick pins into his soul, certainly not a poet's soul. It was of too large an order. Plagiarism was merely a form of Telepathy. Genius did not deal in stolen thoughts.

"Never having loved—" John was right. This love of his and Shelley's, this drunkenness that drowned self and separated soul from body, I had never experienced. It was not the love of mother for child or child for mother: not the love of brothers; nothing paternal about it, or fraternal. It contained no element of superiority or pity. Its heart was equality; sex its soul; and it could only be accomplished by a fusion of two equals of opposite sexes. It was the coming together of two equals of opposite sexes, and in the contact these two, until that time individuals of opposite sexes, yet equals, became fused into one complete, sexless being, losing their own individual identities in one another. The flame of this fusion was Love.

Stranger though I was to Him, I had surely touched the hem of His garment, and so could understand some little something of Him, if I could not take His hand.

And so, materialist by profession, I have ever been on the side of the poets.

XXIX

To follow John was quite useless, I decided. What was to be done would have been done long before I could arrive. And in any case I would not be able to leave until the Saturday. There was nothing for it but to possess one's soul in patience and trust that all would be well.

This I found not easy of accomplishment. Despite the optimistic tone of his letter I was afraid. A capacity for love predisposes a capacity for hate. John was not one of those who "blow neither hot nor cold." He could love greatly, and I was certain that he could as greatly hate. If in loving he could lose himself, he could lose himself in hating. That was what I feared: that he would lose control of himself and do Helga some mischief. And I could not forget his face or the horrid contortion of his hands when we had discussed Helga that day in the hospital.

Two days of suspense passed. Two days when he was scarcely out of my thoughts. I had made up my mind to leave for the Isle of Man on the Saturday as I had originally planned, when a telegram arrived from Liverpool.

I opened it fearfully, expecting I know not what. With profound relief I read:

> Everything O.K. Muriel and I will be with you this evening.—JOHN.

They arrived in time for dinner. John was in the Seventh Heaven; Muriel, sadly altered, grown pale and wan and listless, was as one awaking from an evil dream, semi-conscious, almost stunned, uncertain whether the dreaming or the waking is reality. She recognised me—that was all. Her face as she greeted me was as expressionless as though I had been a mere acquaintance, vaguely remembered.

I was horrified at the change in her. Could this be the same woman who for months had shared my house? Who had been the light of it? Who had radiated love and joy and happiness like a veritable Spirit of Spring? Who had brought Youth to heads grown grey? Who had altered for me the very complexion of the earth?

Could this be the same woman? This semi-dormant, half-dead thing whose hand was ice and whose eyes, half veiled, were like dead moons, not stars. In this woman there was no light, no joy, no youth. A shell walked here, a pale ghost from whom the spirit seemed to have fled in horror at finding itself in such sad circumstances. Alas! Alas! Muriel had gone. And in her place a beautyless thing of skin and bones remained.

Had I taken time for reflection, had I given opportunity to Reason to adjust the balance between sense and the senses, the shock would not have been so excessive. I would have remembered, then, the Muriel that I had first seen, the walking statue as I had termed her. I would have remembered the Muriel we had rescued from the sordid lodgings in Bournemouth. I would have expected that. I would have known that coming thus straight from Helga's hands she must have looked like that. I would have had faith that Love would give her life again.

But the senses were too strong for me. I saw only that the Muriel whom I had grown to—let me confess it—love, whom I love now, was gone. And the sense of something lost was staggering.

No such doubts disturbed John. What he had felt when first he saw the change in her I cannot tell. But now he was aglow with confidence, and treated his wife as though she had been a sick child.

His love was from mine "a thing apart." I knew it as I watched them together. It was of a larger, stronger, wiser order. Compared with mine it was as an oak to an acorn. Where it would have carried him triumphant over the stormiest seas, mine would have—had it not already?—sunk with me. Where mine at first sight had lost faith, his needed no faith, for it knew.

This was Love.

Watching them I felt ashamed, utterly small. John was right. I never had love. Perhaps I was incapable of it. Probably too fond of my own creature comforts, as are the majority of mankind.

Then the wonder of it took me in its hold, lifted me out of myself up to its own level, and unsealed my eyes.

That night I saw—whether a vision or a prognostication of future events I do not know. And I am no visionary, nor yet a mystic. Only I know that I saw:

An altar, sealed with the seal of God, to set it apart from all those others that are but paltry shams. And the flame upon it, now leaping to the heavens as fresh sacrifices were fed to it, now flickering low for lack of fuel, was Love.

And there was no blood upon the altar. All was spotless, white as snow, clean licked, fused white by the flames.

Presently one brought a sacrifice, in itself an insignificant thing, but representing all that that man possessed. Upon the altar he laid himself down. And I saw that it was John.

The flames drew near to him, licked him over, then leaped triumphant. I fancied he was gone; looked to see his smoking ashes; felt myself quake with fear, cried out to him in mortal terror. And lo! I saw him in the midst of the flames, transfigured, radiant, smiling at me, holding out his hands.

That dream I can never forget, so real it was; so reasonable in its significance. And it brought me comfort when comfort was most needed.

After dinner and when he had seen Muriel safely settled for the night, John told me the story of his doings. The difficulty had solved itself in the simplest way. In the late afternoon he had arrived at Douglas, spent the night there, and next morning motored over to Port St Mary. The Fates were with him. Helga had gone out for the day and Muriel was sitting out in the garden. He had merely walked in, and driven away with her.

As the boat did not leave until the following morning, and he was afraid that Helga might follow them and cause a commotion, he had gone with Muriel, the Lieutenant-Governor being away, to the Commandant of the Constabulary and explained matters.

"It was lucky we did," laughed John. "For sure enough the Commandant, an Englishman and an excellent chap, was at the boat himself—to see us off? Hardly; for it was barely breakfast time. He showed me a lengthy screed that had come through by 'phone the night before, from Helga, of course. It was to the effect that her daughter, who suffered from delusions and acute depression, had disappeared. Would he advise the police and have her stopped if she made any attempt to embark?

"I must say I was very thankful when we unhitched hawsers and steamed away. Every minute I was expecting Helga to appear. And then there would have been the devil's own shindy; in spite of the fact that the Commandant stood by—in case of accidents, as he said. He had had a mother-in-law himself, he told me; but not up to the class of mine."

XXX

John and Muriel stayed with me a week. At the end of that time they left for Cornwall, "to put as much distance as possible between that old devil and ourselves," as John explained. Adding: "But for this benighted war we would go abroad—to Honolulu, or some other place beyond her beat. Meanwhile Cornwall is as far as we can comfortably get. We will bide a wee there until the war ends, if it ever does, and if Helga follows us, look out for squalls. I am taking no more chances!"

Their arrangements were carefully made. Even to me their destination was unknown; and they would cover their tracks well, breaking the journey in half a dozen places. Their correspondence would all pass through John's solicitors in London. "We are not even making an exception in your case, my dear old chap," John said as he wrote down the address. "I'm taking no chances whatever. Twice now that woman has nearly killed Muriel; no, not nearly killed, more than killed. For she condemns her to a living death, and that is worse than dying. What her power is and where she gets it, if not from the Devil, I don't pretend to know. But power she has, like the snake over the bird. She has only to look at Muriel to make her quake with fear. She has only to move a finger and Muriel comes. A month with her, and Muriel becomes a living corpse.

"And there is only one person who can stop her, only one person she is afraid of, and that is myself. Because I love Muriel."

I agreed with him. It was far better to take no chances.

So they went away, radiantly happy the two of them, Muriel almost completely recovered, on yet another honeymoon. And as time passed I heard less and less of them.

They found their dream-cottage in the village of "Hush-Hush!" as John called it, "Somewhere" in Cornwall. They sent me a photograph of it. It had the honeysuckle and the jasmine and all the other adjuncts.

A year later I heard that they had a baby girl. "Had it been a boy," John wrote, "you should have been the godfather. You are booked, remember, for the first boy."

An interval of another six months and the photo of the baby girl arrived, still through the firm of solicitors, with a detailed description of her charms.

That was all. Not a word of Helga. Nor had I seen that lady. There was no doubt in my mind but what their troubles were over. And I reflected, not without sadness, that those two were so wrapped up in one another that they would have little room for other friendships.

Then came the sudden ending of the war and the subsequent excitement of peace. And once more I returned to my normal life and bent all my energies upon rebuilding a war-worn practice.

XXXI

Another year had passed. They were still in their cottage of enchantment, and peace seemed to have settled permanently upon them. "I haven't a wish on earth," John wrote, "except perhaps a boy. And I don't think Muriel has either. God has been very good to us."

He had been definitely invalided out of the army and was occupying himself in country pursuits and a certain amount of literary work, which had always been his hobby. I have by me now a manuscript copy of his poems, which I am about to publish. Critics tell me that they are of little account. But I like them, and if I, why not others? The one I quote is called "Contentment," and is typical of those last happy days:

> The race is to the swift, they say.
> Yet we have learned to rest
> Contentedly upon the grass,
> And cheer the runners as they pass.
>   That way is easiest.
>
> For prizes I will not compete;
> What need of prize have I?
> Who sit content upon the grass
> With one who is my own dear lass,
>   Whose only man am I.

The fight is to the strong, they say.
But we have learned that Peace
Cannot be won by ten-score fights,
Nor yet for right, much less for "rights";
    That Love alone brings Peace.

For Heaven itself I would not fight;
What need of Heaven have I?
Who sit content upon God's grass,
With one who is His own dear lass,
    And Love—Himself, so nigh.

And then, like a thunderbolt, the blow fell.

Whether they had relaxed their precautions I cannot tell. It may be that the passage of time had increased their sense of security and made them careless. John's journal would seem to indicate as much. Be that as it may, the first intimation I received of the tragedy came from the daily Press.

A horrible murder had been committed in a Cornish village. An old lady, by name Mrs Helga Stourcross, had been shot dead; and Colonel John Travers, D.S.O., had given himself up to the police and confessed the crime.

The subsequent proceedings, culminating in his execution, are so painful that I cannot bring myself to write about them. The details are well known. Public opinion was all for the poor old woman so foully murdered; and the only excuse that the more generous-minded had to offer was that the man's mind must have been unhinged by his war services.

John, quite obviously, was not insane. As he stood in the dock, erect and quite emotionless, it was patent to all present, to judge as to jury, that he was as sane as themselves.

His counsel—I had procured the best that money could buy, and that in spite of John's protestations—could do nothing. His hands were completely tied by John himself, who insisted upon pleading guilty. "I did it," he said firmly, "and I am prepared to pay the penalty. Believe me, my Lord, and you, gentlemen of the Jury, this was not done hastily, in a sudden fit of anger. It was considered from every aspect. It was done deliberately. The penalty was duly taken into account. In mind I have paid already. I had paid the penalty before ever I pulled the trigger. It remains only for my body to pay. Let there be no miscarriage of Justice under our English Laws, which I am proud to think the finest in the world."

You might have heard a pin drop in the crowded court. Learned Counsel shook their heads. The Judge seemed strangely moved. As for myself, I scarce could contain the tears.

So it was done. What else could be done? Guilty. And then—

I can write no more. The tragedy is too intimate, events are still too green. Let us write only as an epitaph: "He died that another might live."

Thus do great souls go to their God. And we lesser souls remain to do them reverence.

PART II

The Testimony of John Travers

I

My dear old chap,—This disjointed screed, my last epistle to you, will be delivered in due season.

You are not obliged to read it. But if you do manage to wade through these sprawling pages, written as it were from the Edge of the Beyond, you may find something of interest in them.

Why did I kill Helga?

You refrained, most decently, from asking me this question when you came to see me. But I know your intense interest, old chap, in the idiosyncrasies, or what you call complexes, of human character. So here goes.

I killed her because it seemed to me that there was nothing else to do. From the first moment of seeing her in Penzance I knew, intuitively, that the beastly job would have to be done by me. I didn't want to do it. I would have done anything rather than that. To me killing of any description has become abhorrent—I have seen too much of it. You will scarcely believe, after what I have done, that I dislike the idea of killing even a fly. "Kill not for Pity's sake and lest ye slay the meanest thing upon its upward way," has been my creed for some time past—ever since the war.

For weeks I racked my brains as to how I could avoid killing Helga. I made a hundred and one plans. We would go abroad. We would go here. We would go there. But always the result would be inevitable. Helga would follow us "down the nights and down the days... up vistaed hopes... adown Titanic glooms of chasmic fears."

You may say that as once we had avoided her so might we avoid her again. But it seemed to me that there was no escape "from those strong Feet that followed, followed after." It was as though the Sword of Damocles hung over our heads—not mine, I would have laughed at it; but Muriel's.

Had you seen her terror at sight of her mother, it would have wrung your heart—had you loved her as I did. Terror seems a tame word for it. Literally she went to pieces. "She's come! She's come!" was all she could say, in a voice of utter anguish.

Have you ever seen a child in a night terror? She was like that; only the effect was more terrible. For one can wake the child. And when it feels one's arms about it, it is comforted.

Muriel would not awake. From the first moment she went about in a dream; from the expression of her eyes, from the dull horror in her face, most hideous. "She's come! She's come!" she would whisper continuously to me, to the child, to herself.

To me, as you can imagine, it was monstrous, devilish torture. It seemed that nothing that I could do was of any good. Before my very eyes she literally faded away. Not physically only—I could have stood that. More easily I could have seen her die. For, as you know, I have never been afraid of Death; loved him, rather, as a brother who comes to wipe away old age, and ease tired limbs and weary hearts. Always have I thought of him as God's hand, rubbing out regrets, erasing errors, wiping spotless clean our little slates all scrawled with our attempts at Life.

Had Death in his due season come to Muriel, when she had need of him, I would have welcomed him for her. For I know that Death is as much a part of Life as is Birth. That much I know. I know, too, that as Death follows Birth, Birth must follow Death in this stupendous scheme of Life Eternal.

No end to it. One continuous chain, whose alternate links are Birth and Death.

Or we might liken Life to some vast Book; Birth the beginning and Death the end—not of the Book, but of one chapter only. One chapter ended; a page turned; and we begin again—what seems to be a new story. For the Book of Life is like a volume of short stories, a story to a chapter, each one different, each apparently complete in itself. So complete, that enthralled in it we have no memory of what went before. A completely new story; a fresh, clean start, free of everything—old mistakes, ancient regrets, old friendships even.

But between these chapters, between these short stories, seemingly so complete, and maybe in themselves so inexplicable, there runs a vast purpose like a thread of gold. For every chapter, every story is the outcome of its predecessors. It is built upon what went before, like a most subtle novel that step by step, by sometimes straight, by sometimes devious ways, moves to its climax.

This is where Justice enters into this scheme of things, that, as you say, is not sorry, but supremely splendid when one sees it broadly. To fully appreciate the Book and the Master Mind behind it one must read it all. And that, as yet, we cannot do. Our minds are too small to take in more than a chapter.

Torn from the Book, one chapter, ten, may seem sorry, may be sorry. But that represents the whole no more than one birth or ten births and their respective deaths represent Life. One man may be born of low estate and suffer poverty and hardships all his days. Another may be born in exalted circumstances and live all his days in prosperity. That should not make for bitterness. Rather we should say: "That one has earned by his past services exalted state. This one has it yet to earn; let us help him."

This wondrous Book of Life. I, sitting on the brink of Death, seem to see more clearly the vastness of it, its so wondrous wise conception, and its truth and beauty. I see now things that I had never seen.

I see now why we come with memory clean, as clean as though there never had been anything before.

What torture were Eternal Memory! To think and think and think of all our follies, crimes, and cruelties—for ever. That were the blackest Hell of all. But He, that great, wise, loving God, forgets so utterly what we were in what we are, that to Him there is no question of forgiveness. For Him the Present blots out all the Past. He knows that living as we do in Eternal Life we are not fit, as yet, for Eternal Memory. So for all our crimes we come clean into the world, and go out clean for all our crimes.

And yet we pay—to the uttermost farthing. In what we are we pay. And we shall pay in what we shall surely be.

For I know now that Justice rules; is swayed at times, now here, now there, by one thing only—Love; yet still keeps sway. Not as a blind Force or Law immutable—as the Buddhists hold, but as a just Father who is also loving, rules. Justice first. Then Love. This is the order of the Infinite.

Truth rears its tower to the heavens. Each has his own little view of it. For some the barren rock. For others the roses that are climbing here and there. The East has one aspect. The West another. The East sees it as Justice, cold, aloof, like snow-capped peak in June. The West sees it as Love, warm, soft, forgiving—as Jesus was.

Now take these two—more if we can get them; join them; and we have more of Truth.

Call Love the male and Justice the female. Give her the scales—she's juster far than man. Let him be Cupid—the Greeks were very wise. Now mate them. Make them one. And we have Beauty and the *face* of God.

II

Days and nights are nothing to me now. It was last night—or was it this morning?—that I commenced to tell you why I killed Muriel's mother and concluded by creating a Deity. Unlike Kipling's Evarra, however, I do not feel disposed to "cast my God from Paradise." To me He looks good; less austere than the God of the East, and far more reasonable than our Western Triumvirate.

Do you remember discussing the Holy Trinity when we were boys? As far back as I can remember it has always filled me with a certain irritation. To me it has always seemed a sophistry of the most blatant description—a deliberate breaking of the First Commandment and a wordy wriggling to evade the consequences. Jesus Himself gave His interpretation of the "Holy Ghost," which unquestionably had been invented by the priests to mystify the old Jewish faith. The "Spirit of Truth" is at least intelligible to the modern mind. Whereas the other conveys nothing. I remember it used to terrify you.

I grant you that we must have Mysticism. Like Poetry, it is the food upon which our souls must feed if they are not to starve. Take Love. What discussions we used to have about it! But we were fortunate; we had mothers who lived Love.

This mighty force, this mystery that can move mountains, this inner light far stronger than the sun, that every soul can have, yet few know how; this flower of Paradise sprung from God's own bosom, to-day has become a thing to dissect and analyse and laugh at.

To think to dissect this wild, elfin thing of the woods, the silent valleys, and the lonely hills! That flowers only in the great solitudes where man walks hand in hand with God, the father of his soul—or with one woman. Hand in hand, all unobserved, unshamed, and unafraid. So close to Nature, mother of his flesh, that he can hear her heart and read Life's meanings in her mysteries.

Grown thus it flowers, has always flowered, could even be transplanted—anywhere: to any clime, to any conditions, even to the slum of a great city. But there it does not long endure; and seldom, scarcely ever, has been known to flower.

There was one once. A mighty plant, the scent of whose blooms is with us still as a dim, delightful memory.

That one they cut away for fear it would overshadow their Temple and themselves.

Love is Mysticism: Queen of Mysteries. Insoluble by the sage; a living force to its children and by them only interpretable.

To its children—you are one of them, although you have never met your mate, at least not in this life—it gives a sixth sense, X-ray like, that pierces all material forms and reveals the soul of things.

The soul of every single thing—trees, birds, and flowers; and sunsets and sunrises; clouds, trickling water, pattering rain, and the smell of wet dust and new-mown grass.

The soul of a smell? I see you smile—if you have reached thus far and not thrown aside these erratic emanations of a mind, weary and somewhat unbalanced.

For we are all more or less unbalanced, as you used to say: mankind but in its adolescence; and the perfect race a long way from accomplishment. Some—most of us, I fancy—lean too heavily toward the Material; and so lose all Reality. Many others toy too long with dreams; and so lose all Reality.

Impatience, that's the curse of all unbalanced minds. It is our curse to-day—mine, yours, the whole world's, that is, the part that's civilised. One must get back to Nature to procure content; must live a lovely life midst loveliness. For we are not strong enough to stand the stress and strain of this ungodly strife that men call Life. It was not meant for gentlemen. We are not swine to be for ever fighting over the swill bucket.

Some are, you say? Then let them have their fill—of swill. We don't envy them, do we? or covet the swill?

Meanwhile, for all that Death overshadows me, I am content in the "shade of His Hand, outstretched caressingly." Francis Thompson had his sight of Truth. So had Browning: "God's in His Heaven, all's right with the world."

Bless every optimist, say I, who with feet in the mire yet still holds up his head, and scans the sky for stars. And confound the pessimist, who creates most of the mischief here and promptly books it to the Creator's account.

We have one here, a peculiarly unpleasant specimen of the breed. A black specimen—I mean black-coated, dingy of soul as of dress, and with no saving grace of humour. His attempts upon my soul would be amusing were they not so irritating.

But away with him. He has worried me enough.

To return to Muriel—all my thoughts return to her like tired moths. For believe me, dear old chap, I've flitted in the dark. But I can see the light; that's something.

Muriel, since first she saw her mother in Penzance, began to fade. Whether from fear alone, or owing to that strange influence Helga had upon her, I do not know.

With all my strength I fought the accursed thing. Showered love upon her. Never for a moment left her. There was so much at stake—her happiness, the child's, and, incidentally, mine.

She, too, struggled bravely—like a bird in sight of the snare. Times without number she implored me, on her knees, to save her, to save the child. Cried that only I could save them. Then this unholy terror would creep in and clutch her by the heart, and she would say: "She'll win; she'll win. I know she'll win. She always wins."

And she would tell me of her mother's powers, which she seemed to think omnipotent. How Helga was always interested in the occult; had studied it extensively; had travelled after it; and had found— something. How ever since Muriel could remember she had always possessed this—*power* Muriel called it.

What power? you will ask.

There you have me. The thing is utterly beyond my ken. You ought to know, you who have made a life-study of the minds of men. You believe in Suggestion and Hypnotism and all these things, I know. Do you believe in "possession"? Can a person dabbling in the supernatural get into touch with devils and by them be driven, or by them aided, to do the most incredible things?

That is what Muriel believes of her mother. She believed, more than believed, was insistent, that her mother was in touch with something altogether outside herself, a monstrous, evil thing that she could call up at will. She would call it up by going into a trance, and would arise a witch or devil; possessed of such appalling power that she could work miracles—bend people to her will, even at a distance; and if she wished, *destroy* them.

I have heard you speak of "Mass Suggestion," "Telepathic Suggestion," of the power of Love and Hate. I know something of Love's power. But this thing that followed us was incomprehensible, damnable.

At first I laughed at it and Muriel. Then at myself. But laughter failed. For whatever she had or had not done, could or could not do, most certainly Helga had acquired complete mastery over Muriel's mind and instilled in it an unholy terror of herself.

You may imagine that before ever I even contemplated the extreme step of putting an end to Helga's power over my wife and, incidentally, forfeiting my own life, I left no stone unturned. I killed her, as I say, because there seemed no other way of saving Muriel.

Was there another way?

There should have been. There must have been. But I could not find it. Night surrounded me and I could see no dawning. Now I know that Love failed me because I failed, failed in courage. It is always lack of courage that makes us fail. I was afraid to trust my God; lost sight of Him—it was so dark; was impatient of His plans; doubted, fool that I was, that He had any plans. And so I stood alone, with this hideous thing weighing down upon me. No help anywhere but in myself. So took upon myself to break Life's first great Law.

III

Helga. Helga. How I have thought about that woman! Puzzled my brains as to what could have been her motives, first, in permitting me to marry her daughter, and second, in attempting to take her away.

I thought money might have been the first. The second, jealousy.

But who am I, convicted murderer, to sit in judgment upon anyone? What do I know of Helga?

Nothing. To me she is an abhorrence, an enigma. How then can I look into her heart, even were I the most innocent of God's creatures?

Something of her antecedents I do know. It appears that her father was a traveller and student, comfortably endowed with the world's goods, who spent his time in the pursuit of knowledge. A student of Psychology you would have called him. Her mother was a Norwegian, from her portrait very beautiful. They loved each other devotedly it appears. And Helga was their only child.

In course of time she married Stourcross, Muriel's father, a very decent chap, in the 10th Hussars, well connected and all that. So far as one can gather he was a bit wild and somewhat given to lifting the elbow. He died some months before Muriel was born; killed by her mother, according to Muriel. Actually he was thrown by a young mare and broke his neck.

As to Helga herself, you know probably more about her than I do. Undoubtedly she was a strange woman. At times the most brilliant and forceful I have ever met, possessed of most uncanny powers—she could hypnotise, not a doubt of that. I know that she hypnotised me. Times without number those strong, caressing hands have wiped pain away for me. I know that she hypnotised Muriel.

At other times she was the most abject of creatures, dull, careworn, old; and would move about the house or sit huddled by the fire, the picture of misery.

Helga at breakfast and Helga at dinner were two distinct people. Until after lunch she would be the one, abject, pitiable. She would retire then to her room. By teatime she would be transformed.

Muriel always said that she took drugs. It may be so; on the night I killed her she had taken drugs. I know she was fairly partial to absinthe.

Muriel also said that in that interval between lunch and tea she called up her pet devil. This is past belief. On all other points I would take Muriel's word against the world. But so far as her mother is concerned one doesn't know where one is. One thing only is clear—that Helga had the most damnable influence upon my wife.

Helga's appearance in Penzance was quickly followed by one of her peculiarly poisonous epistles to me. It breathed brimstone and hell flames and was freely punctuated with curses, called down upon us in the name of her Deity. At Muriel's request I put it promptly in the fire.

One passage I thought very humorous. To-day it has the nature of a prophecy. "I can see you," it went, "standing on a *scaffold* with a *noose* round your neck. A man touches a button, and you drop— down—down—down—to Hell," or something like that. Anyway, it was realistic.

Then came a perfect bombardment of letters and post cards, addressed in turns to one or other of us. Now she would be vowing vengeance. Now pleading for the poor brokenhearted mother.

We put all on the fire and replied to none. For Muriel insisted that they played an important part in the scheme—for separating us, she said. And she was as terrified of them as though they had been live shells, and would touch them only with the fire-tongs.

Presents for the child came; and were returned unopened.

Never a day passed without seeing Helga's handwriting. Never we went out without meeting her.

One morning, in spite of Muriel's entreaties, I crossed the street to speak to her. She bolted down a side street like a scared rabbit.

This encouraged me. If Muriel was frightened of her, she was certainly frightened of me. I determined to ferret her out, and if possible scare her out of the place.

From the post office I found her address, and that evening went to see her.

She received me as though I had been a surrendered enemy and she a most magnanimous conqueror.

I declined to touch her hand, declined to sit down, and stated my business quite clearly. What did she want? And how much would she take to go away and stay away?

At that she commenced to rave. Said that her daughter was not for sale; that she was not to be bought off; that she had as much right in Penzance as we had—which was true.

"What in God's name do you want then?" I asked.

"My daughter," she said. And poured out a lot of sickly stuff about love. Love, she didn't know the meaning of the word; and I told her so.

She smiled, then, in that hateful, cynical way of hers: "I know your kind of love," she said. "Kisses every day and a child every eighteen months. You men are all alike—humbugs."

"Is your daughter's happiness nothing to you?" I asked.

She smiled again grimly.

"Do you know she is drooping every day from terror of you like—like—" Words failed me.

Again she smiled, as I thought triumphantly.

"So you will not go?"

"No," she replied.

"You will continue to hound us from place to place; continue to make my wife's life a burden to her?"

Her smile made my fingers itch to get at her.

"Then I shall be obliged to kill you," I said, taking a step forward.

At that the smile left her face, and she darted to the door, calling Mrs Something or other—her landlady, I suppose.

I let myself out, and walked home.

Thereafter for two months or so we lived in a state of siege. And day by day Muriel drooped like—I can write the simile now—like a flower before the frost. "She will win," she would keep repeating. "She always wins."

The child, too, became ill. Anaemia the doctor called it and prescribed a tonic. Muriel put it down to a *quilt* that had recently come from the stores, a present so we had fancied from an aunt of mine. The quilt had been on the child's cot. Muriel took and burnt it in the garden. Baby got better.

To such a condition of superstition had my wife been reduced that she imbued even inanimate objects with mysterious powers, and insisted that they were a vital part of her mother's process for destroying her enemies and accomplishing her ends. That they represented *contact*. And that without this contact she could do nothing.

At this time I began to suffer from bouts of acute depression.

Since the war my nerves had not been my strong point. But now a black ominous shadow seemed at times to settle on my mind, blot out all love, all light, all hope, everything worth while, and fill me with hideous forebodings. Fight it as I would, it would keep coming back. At times I would prevail; at other times it would conquer me so completely that I would be as though stuck in a pit so murky that from its depths I could not see one star.

Day by day things became worse—and worse. Here we were, moderately young, devoted to each other, with a most delightful child, and an income ample for all our needs. We were furnished—if ever folk were—with all the furniture for happiness. We had been supremely happy. We would be again—if—if—

If what?

Was it conceivable that one old woman could so upset our world? An old woman who did not even share our home. Could she put out the sun for us? Could she, a ridiculous old woman, steal all the beauty from our land, our sky, our sea? Shatter Love itself with her absurd old hands?

Confounded nonsense! Ridiculous, unreasonable rubbish! And yet—such is the complexity of the human brain—I found myself so thinking—not once, but times without number. And Muriel and I would sit into the small hours discussing this thing that had come upon us. Her fears became my fears. And Helga for us both a grim Demon with all the powers of Satan at her disposal.

Laughable, what?

IV

Some years ago I sent you a photo of our cottage. If you still have it, you will notice in the background another, whitewashed, with a small porch. It was there that I killed Helga.

In the frame of mind in which we then were and which I have attempted to describe to you, you can imagine our feelings when one day we discovered Helga there—next door to us.

We were passing the gate when Muriel caught my arm and cried: "Look there!—at the window."

I looked up—to see Helga leaning out, watching us; on her face that same old evil smile that I have come to associate with her.

Blind fury seized me. Then and there I would have gone to her, dragged her out by the hair, shaken her—shaken her until her teeth rattled in her head, done to her I know not what—had not Muriel fallen in a faint at my feet.

More and more was she becoming addicted to these—heart attacks, the medico called them. But I knew better. It was from sheer terror that she fainted, and usually at sight of her mother, or when upset by some communication from her.

Shaking my fist at the face at the window, I took Muriel in my arms and carried her home. This time sal volatile and brandy both failed to bring her round, and it was two hours before she opened her eyes.

From then on her condition became piteous. Do what I would I could not bring back her wandering mind. For weeks she lay—you have seen her, so you know—in a semi-stupefied condition. The medico could do nothing. A sudden shock, he called it. And plied me with questions which I could not answer.

It was in my mind to telegraph to you. But what could you do? What could anyone do?

The medico recommended a hospital nurse. One came. At first she was most satisfactory. After a time her attitude changed and she began to treat me as though I were a Crippen; doing her damndest to keep me away from Muriel; and even having the impertinence to suggest that I had a bad influence upon her patient.

I could not understand this, until I discovered that Helga had made friends with her, and was taking her out to tea and to the cinema and all that sort of thing; even bringing her home to supper.

The climax came. When I was out one evening Helga came into our house and spent an hour with Muriel and our baby girl.

This I learnt from our little Cornish maid, a loyal soul and devoted to us both.

That same night I gave the nurse a week's wages and saw her off the premises.

Next day our baby, our little Margaret, died in my arms. Thank God, Muriel did not know.

The doctor, sorely puzzled, signed the certificate as death from syncope. I had half a mind to confide in him, but feared that he would suspect my own sanity. Moreover, for some time past his attitude had been anything but friendly. Helga again, no doubt. The woman was implacable.

Then it was that the conviction came to me—not as a mere side-slip of the soul that Reason quickly corrects—but as a concrete issue that had to be faced—I must kill Helga.

*

When we are single how we men laugh at babies! What an absurd little thing is this fragment of blubber and bones that sucks its thumb and slobbers! We wouldn't give twopence for one—when we are single.

Now mate us to the one we love, to her who is our natural complement. Then give us one, O God, or two, or ten. And not all the world's gold could buy one from us.

Surely there is something wonderful about one's child.

It seems to me that children are God's antidote for selfishness. When those helpless little souls are entrusted to one, one cannot be wholly selfish—not if one is any semblance of a man.

For the past hour my warder, an amazing Communist and as amazingly ignorant, has been trying to convert me to his views. He will not listen to reason, has no ideas of his own, and I cannot kick him out. So fly for refuge to the pen and ink.

You remember the New Earth you once drew for my amusement? How I laughed! But that was long ago. You labelled it the Socalist's Paradise.

You had your men and women, I remember, civilised into ladies and gents, so highly educated as to have lost all common sense and reason and the power to think. These you clothed in standard garments from the Common Store. The gents, I remember, wore black togas, and the ladies white—to distinguish them, for in most other respects they were equal. You housed them in standard villas, situated in the straight streets of standard Garden Cities, set out all in squares. They had equal gardens: in front geraniums of the standard red; at the back cabbages from common seed. You also fed them on standard food, balanced rations most scientifically prepared. And, of course, you made them do equal work for equal pay, sleep standard hours, and play for stated hours under strict supervision.

At the psychological age you had them eugenically tested. The unfit were made sterile and so good Socialists. The fit—a few—were mated, scientifically. And the children—here let me add a touch. You made them Common property as all good little Socialists should be. I would have none. For such emancipated people must perforce prefer motor-bikes to babies. And would surely look for salvation, not to Love Incarnate, which is Christ, but to Miss Marie Stopes.

But I am harsh. The warder of my body, who also fancies himself keeper of my conscience, has now gone out, thank God! and I can write: it's folly to be harsh. For everything has its proper place and use. I know that now. Everything has its proper place and use. A mighty thought! that noised abroad would put an end to strife and kill intolerance.

Why cudgel poor Miss Stopes? She has her proper place and use. Good luck to her! For it is well to prevent the unwanted child. In this way only those worthy of propagating their species will do so. And the world will go on getting better.

All is well.

Ours was a child of Love, not Sin. There was nothing sordid or shameful in her conception. Beauty was her birthright, because in her making there had been no ugliness.

From the first moment of her appearance little Margaret had entwined her tendril fingers round my heart; and her welcoming smile had always magic in it.

She was Muriel in miniature, a miniature executed exquisitely; and to us both represented Love's fulfilment in its most perfect form. Her death overwhelmed me; it was so unexpected; seemed so unnecessary. I could see no hand of God in it all—only the bloody hand of Helga. Helga, who had kissed and killed her as would have done a snake.

V

At sight of that dead child the philosophy of a lifetime fell to pieces, and hate—hate of Helga—filled heart and brain to the exclusion of all else. The sight of her, Muriel's baby and mine, lying there so still, so sweet in death, like a flower too early plucked, was sheer torture. Never have I felt such torment.

And from her I would go to Muriel.

And the sight of her, lying there unconscious, moaning feebly to herself, added fresh fuel to the flames that scorched my soul.

Helga. Helga. Helga. The place was full of her. This was her handiwork. And this. And I would look across at the cottage that housed her; look up at the window where we had often seen her watching; and would see—or fancy that I saw—her leaning out, smiling triumphantly at her success and at our undoing.

Believe me, my dear old chap, I did not want to do it. Every hour my heart prayed that the cup might pass from me, even as One long ago in a garden prayed. For Life is sweet, and killing a most horrible business.

But killing there must be, just as there must be wars, in this present state of our development. One could no more imagine the world as it is now inhabited going vegetarian—whether voluntarily or by compulsion—any more than one could conceive of that international bandit, the Bosche, after twenty years' acute preparation for another glorious raid into France, agreeing to Arbitration. The thing is absurd.

Similarly I am satisfied that at this stage of human development—I judge the world to be about eighteen—the death-penalty is essential. This in the circumstances you may think strange, and I know that you, in common with a great many well-meaning humanitarians, are all for its abolishment.

Pour encourager les autres seems to be an all- sufficient reason. The United States has tried the other way, and it has led to a crop of criminals such as the world has never seen. Presently she will retrace her steps.

For myself I am quite prepared to die, for it is just that I should die. I was prepared for the penalty before ever I did the deed that merited it. An argument, you will say, against capital punishment. Not so; for I am no criminal. The criminal is a coward and a sneak, a bully always. Show him the gallows, and he will stay his hand. Show me this side the stake, and this a crown of gold, and I will do whatever I think right.

I die for what I thought to be the right. The issues I weighed carefully, in cold blood. For, thank God, I managed to put hate aside before ever the time came to bury our baby girl.

It was in the evening following the funeral that I reasoned the matter out.

The first question I asked myself was this:—Could Muriel recover while Helga was alive? She had recovered before; why not again? If Love could work miracles, why could it not work them now?

Upstairs I went to Muriel. For hours I tried to call her back to consciousness. For hours I prayed. There was no response. In her eyes no flicker of recognition. There came only from her lips the same low moaning that cut me to the quick.

Looking back now, it seems to me that I failed for lack, not of Love, but faith in the power of Love. It seems to me that I was as Peter on the waves, knowing, yet afraid to trust that knowledge. It was *fear*, I know now; fear of failing, that made me fail.

Helga must die.

I went downstairs again to consider further this matter of life and death.

If Helga died, Muriel would live. She would be alone in the world; she would miss me—terribly. But she was young, unhampered now—a bitter thought, with the best of life before her. Financially she would be quite well off.

If Helga died, she would get well almost immediately—of that I was convinced. And my conviction proved correct, as you know well. Freed from those mysterious mental bonds, she would forthwith become her old self again, be free to live her own life out and to fulfil her destiny.

She must be free, must have her share of Life. And I, from across the Styx, would watch and wait for her; be there to welcome her to the new country when it came her time to cross over.

Helga must die.

I went through my papers and saw that they were in order. I also wrote a note to the doctor informing him of what to expect, and a letter to my solicitors. It was in my mind, my dear old chap, to write to you. For it seemed to me that I, not Helga, was about to die. But on reflection I decided that I should most certainly see you again, and I did not wish to hurt you unnecessarily.

My service revolver was in my uniform case. I took it out and cleaned it carefully, making sure that it was in working order. Then from a box of new cartridges I loaded it.

By this time it was ten minutes to ten. I pulled aside the curtain of the window that faced Helga's cottage and looked out. There was a light in her room downstairs. The rest of the house was in darkness. It would be an hour before she went to bed. Her landlady had already retired to roost.

Again I went upstairs and kissed Muriel good night. This was the hardest part of all.

On the stairs I met the new nurse who had just come in from her evening walk. Something in my appearance must have struck her, for she stopped and enquired about the patient.

"She seems better," I said. "I believe you will soon see a great improvement. Take great care of her, won't you? For I may have to go away to-morrow. Good night."

Slipping the revolver in my pocket I went out, walked quickly to the cottage where Helga was waiting, and looked in at the lighted window.

The curtains were undrawn and she was alone, standing beside the sideboard, an empty glass in her hand. Absinthe, I thought; for she was addicted to it. Then I noticed a small bottle and a jug of water. Drugs, I thought. For Muriel had always insisted that she drugged.

I could have shot her then and there, but reflected that through the window I might miss, and anyway it was cowardly to kill her unprepared. I must give her time to pray, to make her peace with whatever God she prayed to. I must kill her face to face, and tell her why her time had come.

Her face was tragic, ashen, pale as death. Her body seemed quite bent. And she looked old—so old that I almost felt sorry for her. Did she know that Death was so close at hand?

Suddenly she clutched her throat and swayed as if about to fall. Then put down the glass, put away the bottle, sat down to a table littered with papers, seized a pen and wrote a few lines. Then clutched her throat again. She had taken drugs.

A moment later she was sorting the littered papers. Was she writing a book? Drug-inspired, it should make strange reading. Now she was tying them together. Now making a parcel of them. Feverishly, as though she feared the drug would work before she had finished.

The parcel tied, she sealed it with red wax, that in her haste ran down and dropped like blood. Then snatching pen again she scraped the almost empty inkpot, and wrote an address. And before I had time to stir, was out of the room and up the stairs.

Had she gone to bed? Had I missed my chance through waiting like a fool? The lamp was still alight. Would she come down again? Or had her drugged brain forgotten all about it?

I went to the door and knocked.

Would she come down again? Or must I force my way in and kill her in her bed?

I knocked again, and waited.

Footsteps on the stairs. She was coming.

The door opened, and Helga looked at me. Her eyes were wild—with terror.

"I have come to see you on most urgent business," I said.

"Not Muriel? Oh, my God! not Muriel?" Her voice was terrible.

"No, not Muriel. I expect her to be quite her old self again to-morrow. May I come in? I won't keep you more than a few minutes. It is rather important, or I would not have come at this time of night."

She hesitated, and seemed about to shut the door in my face. I was too quick, pushed her back, and closed the door behind me. Then I locked it.

Strangely enough she did not make a sound, only looked at me curiously, almost wistfully.

I seized her by the shoulders and pushed her before me into the room. That door, too, I locked.

Then I took out the revolver.

She looked at it stupidly, with glazed eyes.

"You are going to die," I said. "Kneel down and say your prayers."

And then she became like one possessed. "You fool!" she shrieked. "You fool! You fool!"

"You have one minute," I said.

"You fool! You fool! You fool!" she shrieked, and came towards me with clawing hands.

I pushed her away. "Thirty seconds more," I said.

"Wait! Wait! You fool! You fool!" Her shrieks intensified. She must have been heard a mile away. But ours was the nearest house, and by the time help came she would be past help.

From above our heads came the creak of bedsprings and a scrabbling of bare feet. The landlady getting ready to come down. She would be too late.

Helga, too, had heard it, and commenced to plead for time, hysterically, incoherently. She had something to explain. She must explain. She had—

"Ten seconds," I said.

She sank to her knees then, gibbering.

There I shot her—six times. The first found her head, that cesspit of satanic schemes. She fell back writing horribly. The second I fired into her heart, that harbourage of so much hate. Three, four, five, six shots I fired into her foul body. A few convulsions; and it lay still.

Helga was dead, and her power for evil at an end.

VI

There is little more to write. I walked out unmolested, seeing only a scared face peering over the banisters, meeting no one. It would have been easy to escape.

I was perfectly calm when I entered the police-station at Penzance. The sergeant on duty, with whom I had always been rather friendly, a most excellent chap, point-blank refused to credit my story.

"There! There!" he kept saying, as though to a child. "You just go to bed, sir, and sleep it off. And it'll be all right in the morning. It's them Huns and all you've been through in the war, sir. There! There! Don't you think nothing more about it."

"It's true, man," I said. "And it is your duty to arrest me. You will get into the deuce of a lot of trouble if you don't."

Eventually I persuaded him to leave me by the fire while he went forth to investigate. He point-blank refused to lock me up, and I had the place to myself as he was alone on duty.

Stout chap, Sergeant Johns. A type that only England can produce. Long may he continue to assist the Law and humanise it by his own humanity!

When he returned his appearance was apoplectic. "'Orrible! 'Orrible!" was all he could say.

After the usual rigmarole he took down my statement, which was short. That done, he looked at me most reproachfully, and in silence locked me up.

The rest you know.

*

So it comes to *au revoir*, my dear old friend, my more than brother. *Au revoir*, because we most certainly shall meet again.

How shall I know you in that great Beyond? Your form will most certainly be different. You may have wings, for all I know, and wear a halo for a hat, and be dressed in white, like that angel who hung above our beds when we were boys.

How shall I know you?

I will tell you how. By that ever open mind, so apt to criticise and so alive to truth. By that great big generous soul, all the sweeter for being set within so rough a shell. By that character—yours so splendid—so slowly built up by ourselves in that age-long struggle up the scale of Life, which is the lot of every living thing. With Happiness as bait for our desires and which ensures our efforts to mount up and up—until there comes a time when one's own happiness lures no longer, and Love opens our eyes to the greater end—the giving. The giving up of all—hopes, aspirations, ends, even life itself—to make some other happy. Then we are come very close to God; and His Peace settles down upon our souls, even though men call us criminal and our end, so far as they can see who have no sight, the gallows.

By these signs shall I know you. By these signs shall you know me.

We shall not rush into each other's arms. No hasty judgment shall surprise me into saying: "This is you." But when my mind reads yours aright, then shall my soul say: "This is you." And once again we shall be friends.

I have just seen Muriel for the last time. I was writing this when she came in. She read the last few lines, and wept; and then was glad.

Help her, old friend. Hers is the hardest part. God bless you both.

JOHN TRAVERS.

PART III

The Soul of Helga Stourcross

I

It is very early. The sun is just coming up. To-morrow at this time I shall be dead.

Before night comes, I must finish this—for you, try to make you understand. Then I shall pull my bed over to beneath the roof-window in the thatch, so that the stars are the last thing in this life that I can see... I do not mean to wake up any more.

I used to go to sleep like that, long ago in childhood, in that other little room under the roof at home. Lying there in my bed at night, the stars were the last thing I used to see. Sometimes they were clear and shining, and then I pretended they were my mother's eyes looking at me out of Heaven... sometimes they were misted over, as if those same eyes were full of tears...

At the cottage over the way, all the blinds are drawn... They have been drawn for two days. They bury the little thing at two o'clock.

Before night comes, I will have finished this. I will have put it where my landlady will find it when she wakes in the morning. I have written her instructions. She is to keep it for a year, and then send it to you.

In a year you will not hate me quite as you do now. She will carry out these instructions to the letter. Even if there is an inquest, no coroner will be able to drag it out of her. And this not because she has any honour or loyalty about her (that class never have), but because she *dare* not disobey me. On the envelope I will tell her exactly what will happen to her if—a moment before the year is up—she gives this to a living soul.

She will know that I can make it happen. She suspects, by now, a little of the power I have. She guesses something of what I can let loose upon her. She is horribly afraid of me, like John Travers, and Toogood, and the rest of them. Like Rupert was before he died, and my father, and you, and little, little Helga... oh, my God, what I have suffered... what I have suffered...

She dare not give me notice, or she would not have kept me here a day. The fool dare scarcely bring my meals in. While she puts my tray down she is staring round into the corners, and backing, with that stupid, conciliating smile of hers, towards the door. What does she think she sees, I wonder? Or is It grown so incarnate now, that even these insensitive serfs can see It and shudder away?

That long, long Shadow, drinking up the sunlight. That long, long Shadow, filling all my room... But to-night I shall defy It... I shall do to-night what surely none yet has dared to do.

I defied God once, and all the powers of His Heaven. And when His lightnings fell upon me I did not repent. Why repent at punishment? Cravens do that, and churls. Not I, who have in my blood the fire of the old Norwegian kings. Shall I bow the knee to a power which strikes me, or submit meekly to that which heaps suffering upon me? No. I cursed God in His place, and did not die.

I cursed Him because He had made me love a man who could not love me. Because He had filled my heart full with that terrible fire which if it overflows not, creates not, burns the soul away. Because He had made me so that to gain Rupert's love I would—did—go to Hell. Because Rupert, when he knew what I was, turned from me in despicable fear.

Once then, I defied God and all His Heaven. To-night I will do a greater thing. Shut out of Heaven and claiming naught from God, I set at variance all the powers of Hell.

Once I am dead, that long Shadow in my room will lengthen till it encompasses me utterly, absorbs me completely. When It and I have gone, the world that knew us will be clean again.

Clean as the sands are when the tide has gone out. Clean for you, for John, for the children that will come to you.

You will be able to live and love and laugh unafraid.

There is a verse that runs in my head. It is somewhere in the Bible:

"There shall be a way—the unclean shall not pass over it... it shall be for those... though fools, they shall not err therein."

Have any of those ignorant slaves who call themselves orthodox believers realised the wonders of their accepted Book?

"Though fools, they shall not err therein. There shall be a way—"

I shall not pass over it. But you will, and John, and your children. Because, in defiance of all the powers of darkness, I shall have set the gate of it ajar for you.

My mother was the loveliest woman I have ever seen, and she and my father the only perfect pair of lovers I have ever met.

She was Norwegian; tall, slender, with the delicate limbs of a Greek goddess and a literal crown of pale gold hair. Her face was pale, too; and her eyes—Rossetti, my father said, was describing eyes like my mother's when he wrote of those

> "deep pools
> of waters stilled at even."

They were like that, deep, limpid, dreamy, mirroring the things of Heaven.

She died when I was nine, so nearly all that I know of her actual self was taught me by my father, who represented her to me as a faultless angel. Himself the only really good man I ever met, he saw everything, as I suppose good men will, with a sort of idealised vision. He used to tell me that he loved my mother above all for her goodness. But I know now that no man loves any woman for her goodness. So he really loved her for her exquisite shell, her eyes, her crowning hair, her magical voice, her walk, her smile... He loved her for her gaiety, her wit, her brilliance. For my mother had the intelligence of the Northern women. Wherever she went she must have shone. In whatever group of women he saw her, my father could never have failed to feel that thrill of pride in her which men *must* feel for the women they love, if that love is to remain alive.

As my father always sought truth and loved goodness, my mother was a mirror of truth and goodness. For she loved my father as such women do, with a love far stronger than death. Since he so valued goodness, she was good. Since he so valued truth, her every thought was true. She would have been burnt at the stake sooner than disappoint him. As she kept her body beautiful to delight him, as she kept her brain fine and subtle to enchant him, so she kept her soul exquisite to sustain him. Not the least thing my father loved her for, though he never knew that, was her marvellous and overwhelming love for him.

In such a devotion I was naturally a shadowy third, but it was happier to be the shadow of such a pair than the pampered darling of an ordinary bickering, selfish couple. I grew up in the belief that a great love for a noble man is woman's rightful inheritance, a destiny for which she must develop herself, perfect herself, make and keep herself worthy... Subconsciously, this pure ideal became woven into my being, and when the time came for vague dreams of love, it was of a knight very true and splendid, without fear and without reproach, a Bayard, a Galahad, of whom I should be the inspiration and the reward.

Of course, he had the face and form of Rupert. Shelley says that those who grow together when they are children cannot choose but love each other later on. We grew together, solitary children both, for our places were only divided by a boundary hedge. But we were, in all things else, very different. Rupert was adventurous and brave, dark-haired, dark-skinned, dark-eyed. He was strong and healthy, vigorous and impatient, resentful of control, impulsive, sometimes violent. I was a very delicate, very sensitive, very gentle little girl. Fair, wistful, full of fancies—some beautiful, some morbid, others wild and sad and strange and gay.

I did not know then that I was a medium. My father, absorbed though he was in Spiritualism, never suspected it. He investigated Spiritualism, as everything else, with that single-minded searching after truth which characterised him; not as my mother had, to establish a link which, even if death parted them, should hold his soul to hers.

He believed he talked with her in those séances he held, and that she revealed to him, like Dante's lady, things concerning the spheres where she awaited him. He believed he saw her, as in that poem of Rossetti's which he always called her portrait

> "leaning out
> from the gold bar of Heaven."

I dare say he was partly right. Any vision of my mother in another life must have revealed her watching him, loving him, guiding and shielding him with her prayers. But I feel sure she would never have gone on into any Heaven without him. I can rather picture her waiting at those gates of Death through which one day he must surely also come.

If I had known I was a medium, I should have known the reason of some of my odd fears. As it was, I feared the dark without knowing why, and the twilight before the stars came out, and old shut-up houses, and long-ago lived in, unused rooms.

I was so dreamy and imaginative that when Rupert was away at school and I had no one to play with, I peopled the old house with bright beings to keep me company. Angels, which nurse had read to me about; and jolly little elves and pixies who laughed at me round corners, and my dear mother, whose eyes (I pretended) were the stars peeping down at me at night; and a host of splendid figures from the old stories of chivalry and romance. I chattered to Charlemagne and King Arthur; Siegfried told me new and strange adventures; I related these aloud to the pixies most dramatically, pretending that Siegfried was declaiming at my elbow. I brought in the old gods and heroes of my mother's people. Among them all, perhaps, the best-loved figure was little English Una, walking through the world to find her knight, in her white gown and naked feet.

I let nothing into my make-believing that was not bright and lovely. Morbid fancies I had, too, but when alone I chased them away. They frightened me. They were fun to scare Rupert with; for I knew I could scare him, for all his pooh-poohing. I did not want to be scared when I was quite alone.

Yet, across my waking, across my sleeping, I sometimes felt the Shadow.

This was a most strange feeling. Perhaps I would be playing happily at my pretendings, in the old panelled hall or at the foot of the wide staircase. And suddenly an uneasiness, a chilliness, would creep over me. My bright companions would become unreal and fade from me. I would feel alone, terribly alone—yet not alone.

For somewhere in that hall, invisible but watching me, I would become conscious of a Something that sent me sick with fear.

It was vast and very strong. It was dark and very sinister. It was older than my heathen gods, and It knew more than all my ancient bards could sing about. More of life and death, and passion and pain, and madness and misery, and utter, utter wrong.

At Its passing the breathing grew shallow and the heart grew faint. At Its passing, the sunlight became twilight and the birds became still. That awful, icy quietness (which since I have come to know so well) would make the ticking of the clock seem terrifyingly loud.

Then I would cry: "Oh, please, Our Father! Kind Jesus! Oh, my own mother, send It away!"

It would vanish like a dream. There would be the hall, flooded with sunlight and bright with rugs. The pictures, the weapons, the streak of light from the stained-glass window upon the white wall. And I still trembling in the warm sunshine, still murmuring:

"Oh, please, please, don't let It come back any more!"

Ah! No such prayers now will drive It away from me—who have done with God, done with love, done with hope. Whose hands, in a few hours, lay hold on Death, whose feet go down to Hell.

The days went by and became weeks; the weeks went by and became months; the months went by and became years; while I played on in the garden of my dreams.

Rupert was but seldom in the garden, as far as his visible self was concerned; he was being educated at one of the great old English schools; later he went to Sandhurst; his mother, a wealthy widow, had a passion for travel; and as he grew older even his holidays and vacations were chiefly spent abroad.

But his spirit stayed with me; the brave figures of my knights and heroes all wore his form: I invested him with all virtues, all gifts and graces possible to man or boy.

When I was nearly eighteen Aunt Elizabeth swooped down like a hawk into my garden.

She was full of reproaches for my father, contemptuous expressions for me—here I was, nearly eighteen, at an age when she herself had married, and married, too, the most eligible *parti* of her season. Here was I, untravelled, uneducated, a gawkish ill-mannered child, with flaxen pigtails, and great eyes staring surprisedly at her like a cow! No manners, no *savoir-faire*, no idea of dress or deportment, no knowledge of the world! What was my governess doing? *Who* was my governess? Why had I not been sent abroad, had the corners rubbed off, been taught how to comport myself in the great world? Why was I not out? Did not my father intend to give me a London season? I should be now dancing my way through a maze of balls and parties into the good graces of my future husband. A great deal of what she said was quite untrue, for I was not uneducated. I was widely read, not only in the literature of my own country, but in that of at least two others. I read French and German fluently, I knew Latin and a little Greek. My father had introduced me to and given me a love of many strange ologies and sciences; but in all the things in which Aunt Elizabeth excelled I was an ignoramus. Of all the things in which she had tutored her own daughter Dolores I had never even heard.

I had never learnt to dance. I could not play either mandoline or banjo. Though I had lingered raptly with my father in many famous picture-galleries, and could pick out an exquisite sculpture at a glance, I had never learnt to fiddle with sketch-block and brushes, or "do" crystoleum or torture bits of ribbon and silk into hideous embroideries. I had never learnt to talk, with pretty smiles and blushes, strings of aimless conventionalities for hours at a stretch. My waist was wrong, my feet were wrong, my postures were wrong, my questioning gaze was wrong... How my father ever expected a girl so gauche to find a husband Aunt Elizabeth did not know.

All that she said greatly upset my father. He, poor man, adrift in his memories or occupied with his strange studies of strange mysteries, had completely forgotten that I must find a husband... I can imagine how he must have tried to vindicate himself, and I know, from what happened later, that he said he had always thought (when he had thought about it at all) that I would some day marry Rupert and so it did not greatly matter.

And who was this Rupert? demanded Aunt Elizabeth. Was he well connected? Wealthy? A suitable match? Where was he now? When had he last been here?

Very well connected. Quite well off. Five years older than I, therefore most suitable. Where was he? Oh, with his regiment. Been here lately? Well, no; not since going to India three years ago. But when he came home, of course—

With such complete folly Aunt Elizabeth was exasperated... Two children, playing together because they have no neighbours—and on that a sentimental fool rests all his hopes for his daughter's future! When I came out, this Rupert should certainly be encouraged, and it might come to something. But not if I were as I was now. *No* young man of good prospects and in a smart regiment would *look* at such a girl as I was now.

Aunt Elizabeth took me away with her, of course... My father was convinced that he had behaved with criminal negligence and folly. She took me away to her London house, and with Dolores she endeavoured to train my feet to walk upon the way that they should go. She plied me with visiting-masters and mistresses. We "did," with our completely cynical finishing-governess, everything that ought in such circumstances to be done. The books I loved were removed from me—if not definitely immoral they were considered at least unsuitable for next season's debutante... The lightest and most worthless novels were fed to me instead. At last I sickened of them and would not read them, these stories of women who became engaged from pique and married from misunderstanding; who, artlessly artful, played one suitor to entangle another; who inveigled hearts with their babyish prattling, and tied strong men up in the knots of their kittenish wiles.

Dolores I hated. She was the first person I had ever hated; and I hated her so intensely that I think, though incapable of real feeling, she presently grew to feel for me an emotion as near hatred as any that *could* dwell in her shallow and futile soul...

She was very pretty, in a Frenchified kind of way. Her dark hair was always perfectly done, her slim figure corseted and padded until it was a fashion-plate. Her neck and arms were beautiful, her eyes very soft and sly; she prattled, she blushed, she dropped her eyes, she lifted her eyes; she was so modest that nearly everything shocked her; she wore her dresses cut so low that the sight of them shocked me.

She thought Shakespeare coarse and Dante "too weird." She secreted low French novels in her room and read them in bed at night, after kneeling down, a devout white figure, to say her lengthy prayers.

I hated her.

But I know now that those are the women men find irresistible.

I used to lie awake in my own bed, when at last she put the candle out—I used to lie there, after the futile, heart-wearying, worthless day, and try to build up my soul again with dreaming of the mighty ones I knew.

Splendid kings and warriors; wives faithful beyond death; knights who rode through fire to win a bride all glorious within.

Bah!... I know now that they are all dead, the old heroes, the old gods... The men of our day choose their loves from prostitutes, and their wives from treacherous, simpering dolls.

*

I did not meet Rupert until the night of my coming-out ball. He had only just returned to England, and I had not seen him for over four years.

I was wildly excited. Aunt Elizabeth had told me he had been invited and had accepted. She had told me, too, that she had made careful enquiries about him, and that she had ascertained that he was in every way a most suitable young man for me to marry.

She informed Dolores, in as exact terms, of four men who were to be present who were equally desirable for her to marry. One, I remember, was an old roué of seventy-two, who looked like Voltaire. Another was a semi-imbecile youth who, by some extraordinary freak of fate, was heir to a noble name and many acres.

I had chosen my own dress for this occasion. Aunt Elizabeth had not approved of it. But even she, when I had it on, had to admit that it suited me. I was not pretty, but I had inherited a few of my mother's beauties. The fine gold hair that this night (in defiance of all fashion) I wrapped around my head like a crown. The large eyes, so much lighter than my mother's that whereas hers were deep pools, mine were more like clear, shallow lakes. The pale skin like the petals of a creamy rose.

I wore a frock that, in those days of waists and hips, was a straight slip that fell from shoulder to hem. It was, in a day when every debutante wore white, of shimmering golden tissue, that gleamed and rippled as I moved.

My slim white arms hung bare without a bracelet. I wore no rings. Those chains and gewgaws are for slaves. For such were they originally made, and of such they remain symbolic.

Would Rupert remember, I wondered, that it was in a golden gown that the daughter of kings (in the old Northern legends) came forth to her betrothing?

He remembered something, for the first thing he said to me which I heard clearly, was:

"Is it a heathen goddess, or what?"

"Perhaps," I answered. He laughed immoderately.

"Great Scott, what a kid you were in those days! Talk of fairy-tales. You could give one the creeps sometimes, in a way surpassing the Divine Sarah! Are you as bad still?"

"Perhaps," I answered. A strange trembling had seized me, and something was beating in my throat like a bird. There was a mist around us. The bright lights were dim. A long, long crying was coming from the violins, sweet as Life is, sad as Death is. Rupert's arm went round me, and we swept out together across the floor.

Oh, what a fool I was! What an utter, utter fool!

At first, as we floated away together (he danced wonderfully, and so, by now, did I), he talked to me about all sorts of trivial little things. I answered vaguely "Yes," "Yes," "I think so," "Perhaps," "Yes."

I wished he would not keep on talking. I wanted to listen to what the real Rupert had to tell the real me.

Presently he did stop talking.

It seemed to me that then at last I could hear what he was telling me. How he had missed me, how lacking in life and savour all the things had been which he had done without me, what wonderful things we would now do together. We would fly out into the sunlight together—always together, always in the sun. Fly to the lands where dwells beauty old and new; across strange seas, across strange deserts, to marble palaces set amid cool waters; always together, always in the sun.

He had grown very splendid to look at. As dark, as eager, as impulsive as ever, but more gay and debonair. He danced the whole evening. Once I passed him on the stairs with Dolores. He was laughing and talking as if it were twelve o'clock instead of half-past two.

He danced a great deal with Dolores. She was more coquettish and sparkling than I had ever seen her. Old Voltaire became positively senile. Even her imbecile boy woke up. That night I did not hate her any more. My heart was full of pity for her. If she had had some one splendid like Rupert to love, everything would have been different for her too. If—

It was the last dance of all. I had kept it for Rupert, and the first notes were beginning. My former partner had left me with my chaperon, but as that chaperon was Aunt Elizabeth, she was now called away. I heard Rupert's voice on the other side of the palms. He was coming to look for me.

No he was not. He was bringing Dolores back to Aunt Elizabeth. He was picking up something she had dropped—a white wisp—and giving it to her. Their hands and heads were touching. She was looking up and looking down, teasing, pretending, encouraging—

I collected a lot of quite useless trifles very carefully—bouquet, programme, fan. I went to the cloak-room and found my golden cloak and sat down by the fire. I was so dreadfully cold. I kept on seeing Rupert's face as it had looked, smiling down at Dolores.

No one noticed me. The waltz was half over. Footmen were already calling up the carriages.

A week or so went by. Rupert was always at the house. He was at the dances where we were to be. It was not for my sake he came—I think he scarcely knew if I were there or not.

I scarcely knew myself if I were there or not. Part of me sat there, embroidered, sketched, was tried on, danced, and played. Another part of me was in a place apart, a place cold and void with high winds sweeping through it, crying aloud to God through the night and through the day.

"Make him love me! Make him love me!"

But her hold grew tighter.

As I danced and walked and ate, even as I slept, that other part of me continued its sobbing to its Maker.

"Separate them! He is not hers, but mine! She does not love him—anyone else would do as well. For me there is no one else."

But God did not hear me. Perhaps, like that lesser god of old, He was hunting, or He was sleeping. Or perhaps the loves of this world were a weariness to Him, since all the great lovers had left it long ago. I should have left it, too—why had I not? For what sin was I chained relentlessly to this earth, dancing to its foolish piping, listening to its shallow merriment? I would finish with it. I would kill Rupert and myself; set him free, even if he did not desire to be set free. Once dead, he would understand. Once dead, our souls would rush together; and then we would fly on and on, as we had done to the crying of the violins, but never to be separated any more.

You will say I was mad. No doubt I was. All lovers are mad. All genius is mad. There is a fire at the heart of things that burns very fiercely. Some of us have come too close to it. That is all.

A strange thing began to happen to me.

You remember that I told you how, long ago in childhood, a recurring experience used to frighten me? You remember that invisible Something which used to manifest itself to me?

I became aware of It again.

At all sorts of odd times. In brilliantly lighted ballrooms; in faintly lit conservatories; suddenly hushing the babbling voices round me at a dinner-party—by that awful, icy quietness, by that sense of darkness, I would know that It was there.

Never visible, never tangible; but *there*.

In the old days, sick with fear, I had cried out for salvation from It to all the powers of good I knew.

But now, shuddering and cold, I yet did not put It away. A strange thought was with me. That there was some link between That and myself. That It watched me from Its distance, desiring to make the distance less. That if I so willed, *I* could make the distance less.

And It was wiser than my heathen gods. It knew more than all my ancient bards could sing about.

It knew how to accomplish all which I and my prayers could not accomplish. Its soul, overshadowing mine, could obtain for me what mine alone would never obtain.

And Dolores, looking up and looking down, wore the roses that Rupert sent her, and that Voltaire sent her, and that the imbecile boy sent her, by turns.

And Rupert, distracted and enchanted, became more distracted and enchanted day by day.

And I did not pray to God any more. I whispered in my soul to Something Else instead.

II

Zinera was the popular medium of that day.

Perhaps I did not tell you that Spiritualism, as revealed in table-turning, Ouija-boards, and séances, was *the* fashionable amusement. Some people took it seriously. My father had... The rest regarded it as something new and vaguely naughty which did not upset any conventions. In many houses where we went, table-turning was a regular Sunday evening entertainment. Mediums were in great demand, and were therefore, for the most part, worthless charlatans.

But my father had employed Zinera, and spoken highly of her psychic capacity and her honesty. I had seen her at my own home, a middle-aged, very fat woman, with luminous, blind-looking eyes.

With Thérèse, Aunt Elizabeth's maid, I went down the steps of the Pont Street house one dull October afternoon. I wanted a walk, I said. And she, annoyed at being made to walk when we could so easily have driven, accompanied me with bad grace. At last, irritated by the creature's complaint about her ridiculous shoes, I hailed a hansom, and handing the cabman a slip of paper on which an address was written, bade him drive us there.

I would have preferred to walk, for my brain was in a turmoil, and the cool air and bodily movement might have calmed me. But it would have taken us too long. Zinera lived in Maida Vale.

She lived in a gloomy house of which every window was heavily curtained—mediums usually live in houses like that. It gives them an air of mystery. A dark man who could not speak English opened the door and showed us into a room so hung with fusty draperies that it almost choked the breath... After a long time the door opened and Zinera came in.

I bade Thérèse wait, and followed the medium into a room even darker, stuffier, and more dusty than the one I had left. There was, I remember, a large, malevolent-looking portrait of Madame Blavatsky over the mantelpiece, and a fat puppy in a basket near the door. On the table lay paraphernalia of the craft, a crystal, a shallow bowl of water, and some books with curiously wrought bindings. It was depressing in the extreme.

She had the smooth, soothing voice that I have noticed in priests and mediums—the voice of a person used to frightened credulous people, and cultivated, not to dispel their fear or lessen their credulity, but to increase both to complete abnegation.

I looked her between her unseeing eyes and said:

"I want to get in touch with some one."

"Yes, yes," she crooned.

"I don't know whether I can or not. No, that isn't true. I know that I can, but I am afraid to do it alone. Will you help me? Will you show me how to get in touch with it at any time and not be afraid?"

She took my hand and began to make little movements with her other one. The room was so still that the distant roar of traffic came to us faintly as from a world left behind. Minutes passed, and she breathed slowly and deeply.

I watched her. She was lying back in her chair, her eyes open. The stillness in the room was not the stillness which had been there before. The darkness in the room was not the dimness which had been there before.

I could see her face, white and puffy against the gathering gloom... The room was very cold. I could hear the sounds of distant London no more; but other sounds, strange indeed in that place. The feet of a multitude passing slowly to the throbbing of a muffled drum. The sound of running waters purling clearly. Piercingly high and sweet, the sound of singing voices borne along upon a wailing wind.

The wind seemed to be in the room, too. I could hear the curtains swishing and the blinds rattling. I could hear things being lifted and thrown down again. But I could see nothing, for the darkness was now complete.

Then the wind died down to a little gentle sobbing, and I knew that three sat where before there had been but two.

Rushing waters were pouring into the room, lifting me till I must needs get upon my feet. I stood up, swaying and gasping. It was dark no longer. An intense and blinding brightness was above and around me, too dazzling to be borne. Out of the brightness I heard words spoken. I did not know then, nor do I know now, what they were. But I knew then, and I know now, that they were too terrible for human consciousness to understand. I knew no more.

When I opened my eyes again the room was just as it had been when I had first entered it, with the exception of Zinera, who was leaning forward in her chair watching me, an expression of horror upon her puffy face.

Blavatsky over the mantelpiece, crystal, books, and a now empty dish of water on the table. Stuffy, sordid, dusty, depressing.

I heard some one laughing, and for a moment did not realise that it was myself.

"You should have told me," the woman said, "that you were a medium."

I? A medium? Scarcely. An enchantress, perhaps, to whom strange powers had been given. I needed only to lift a finger and Zinera would turn and run from the room. The thought gave me great pleasure. Such power as I now felt within me was a thrill in the veins. How delightfully one could make people suffer!

I went on laughing at this new possibility in life which I had discovered. To be able to make things suffer! That, indeed, was a diversion for the gods. I understood at last what exquisite pleasure the cruelty, injustice, and misery in the world must provide for the powers that be. Yet there were people who hoped for a Millennium, and a Heaven of harmony and love. Foolishness!

The smoking black blood of slain beasts upon their altars; the screaming of rivals tearing out each other's throats; all the tears and anguish and hate and cruelty and fierce desire which had rolled down the centuries—these were the things that made one laugh in sheer joy to think of them—made one go on laughing and laughing—

"Drink some water," whispered Zinera. Her voice was hoarse and trembling. "For the love of God, try to regain your control. Concentrate... breathe deeply..."

"On the contrary," I said, "I have never even dreamed of attaining such control as I have now. I can control lives, destinies. Yourself, for instance. I could, at this moment, take and shatter—"

"For the love of God," quavered Zinera, "breathe deeply—drink water—"

"Don't be alarmed—I don't intend to do you any harm. I am too anxious to know what actually happened. You went into a trance, didn't you? And did anything come?"

"*I* went into no trance," said Zinera. "But you did—almost immediately."

"And—"

"It came. Almost immediately." She looked at me.

"And what happened? How long did It stay?"

"It has not gone away," said Zinera.

"What do you mean?" I said. I cannot describe the terror and triumph that I felt.

"It is still here," said Zinera. "With you. You are a most powerful medium."

I began to mock her fiendishly.

"And who," I asked her, "is this familiar? It seems to cause you uneasiness. I suppose Its ways and manners are not quite those of the spirits at your fashionable séances? More elemental, perhaps? More powerful? What exactly do you suppose It to be?"

She looked at me and gibbered.

Presently, still laughing, I threw two gold pieces into her lap and left her.

As I went to the door, my eye fell on the fat puppy in its basket. Something in its attitude struck me as peculiar. I bent over and touched it. Then I saw that it was dead.

At dawn, when the light came in and a little wind blew along the streets, the Thing left me. At the beginning It always did that. It frequently does it even now. As the light grows and I hear that little wind rising, It often leaves me and I fall asleep.

The waking is the worst. I wake weak as water, bereft, trembling. That first morning, as on others since, I looked at myself in the glass and was appalled. My face was chalky, my lips grey, my eyes staring. I might have been drugged. I pulled myself together. I remembered all that had happened. This Thing should not kill me until It had given me my heart's desire.

I rang for Thérèse, breakfasted, had my bath and dressed. I never, from that time on, appeared downstairs till luncheon. No one thought this in any way remarkable, as I and Dolores seldom went to bed before three in the morning. I no longer shared a room with Dolores. I had asked for one of my own.

Every afternoon, as the early dusk crept on, I called It back. It always came.

Usually in the same manner. I sat quietly, my hands clasped, calling It in my soul. I always sat at the same hour; and I always, as that fearful brightness succeeded the gathering darkness, heard those incomprehensible words spoken that blotted out my consciousness.

The whole thing was very rapid; when I awoke, I usually found that less than half an hour had elapsed since I had sat down in the chair.

I sat down in that chair a shivering, resolute girl. I rose from it a Circe, a binder of souls.

I rose from it wise with the wisdom that destroys. I knew things. The thoughts of those I went among were open to me, and they amused me mightily... I amused them mightily, too. People began to talk to Aunt Elizabeth about her brilliant niece.

It gave me a sort of beauty, too. It lit up my eyes and hair and clear pallor till they were all glowing... Even my white throat and arms shone. I looked like a strange flower lit up from within by a lamp.

I knew things. How to entice and lure, how to draw people towards me. How to cause strange hurts and injuries to people... Over certain minds my power was far greater than over others. And I found women less easy to subdue than men.

Circe-like, I delighted in reducing men to folly. I loved to see their centuries of civilisation fall from them at my will. I liked to call out the wild beast in them which the world likes to think was outgrown long ago. I would have loved to set them at each other's throats, tearing and rending, and watch the life-blood of the vanquished pouring out upon the floor. I would have loved to hear the sobbing of the women who cared for them, and of whom these madmen thought no longer, since their brains were crazed with the thought of me.

But I did not allow these ideas to sway me. I knew from whence they came; and since I controlled this mighty Thing, could call It to me at will, and if I so willed, refrain from calling It; since, in short, It was my Servant and not my Master, it was for me to limit Its outrageous desires.

I did, however, draw husbands from the wives who loved them, and make them laughing-stocks; and when they were lost to all sense of honour and manhood, destitute of pride, mock them and pretend amazement at their effrontery... One lad, engaged to a girl I knew who would have died for him, blew out his brains when he knew what he was and what I was. He had a young, beautiful face. I have often seen it since in dreams.

Rupert was the easiest of all my victims. He became mine more completely than I had ever in wildest dreams imagined him. Ambition left him. *Savoir-faire* left him. He neglected his work. He neglected his play. Dolores was forgotten. He thought of but one thing and that was me.

I delighted in torturing him, playing with him. I delighted in torturing Dolores. As much as she could care for anything, I believe she cared for Rupert. I loved to watch her face those nights, as we danced the short hours away.

Then home. To strange, wild waking dreams that flew around my bed like fiery birds. Dreams so fearful, so ecstatic, so beyond human word to describe, that I would sit up screaming out with laughter in the darkness.

Till the little chink of grey would show above the blind. Till the little dawn wind would move the curtains.

Then I would bury my face in my pillow and sob and sob and sob.

No enchantress then: but a girl terrified, wretched, forlorn; who had done with good, and yet most intensely hated evil. Who had set a human love beyond good and evil, and who, at the bidding of neither God nor Devil, would relinquish her human love.

In May I married Rupert. Dolores was my only bridesmaid. In June she was to be married to Voltaire.

I will never forget that morning. I awoke earlier than usual, after a night of horror which was worse than anything I had yet experienced. I woke to the sweet sunlight of a six o'clock May morning.

Getting up, I crossed to my window and leaned out. The tall London houses, usually sombre and dark, were flooded with gold. The extraordinary sweetness and cleanness of the world brought tears to my eyes. Not the tears, bitter and hopeless, that I nightly shed. But tears that gushed out as if an angel had touched a spring of healing in my soul and bidden the waters rise and flow.

I thought:

"Need I go on?"

If only Rupert had been different! If only the man I loved could have loved me for what was best in me! If only he had loved me for what was fine in me!

Oh, Man, Man, how hard you have made the way for Woman if she loves you! That being, meant to be so beautiful, given to you long ago in Paradise. How ill you have cherished her—along what stony roads you have driven her.

I leant my head on the sill and cried and cried. And thoughts spoke in me, lovely thoughts, like the whisperings of a guardian angel.

If Rupert had only been charmed by Dolores because he had never learnt to know the real me! If now, having won him, I could cleanse my soul again, cleanse it of all which had polluted it, make of it a clear depth into which my lover might gaze and never wish to look away! If I could teach him to love me for all the beautiful things that grow in women's hearts for the men they love! As my father had said he loved my mother—more than for all her charm and beauty—because she was so good!

I knelt on, and the sunlight strengthened, and I could feel it like a kind warm hand on my hair... I knelt on, reaching out towards that warmth and tenderness, towards that kindness—

Thérèse tapped at the door. I opened it. My face must have looked different from the one she had seen these many mornings past.

"Leave me," I said. "Do not come for me until I must be dressed."

"But mademoiselle must eat something!"

"Leave me," I said. "Come for me at the last moment possible. I am at prayer."

She looked at me searchingly, crossed herself, and went away.

I did not see the crowd of people as, later, I passed up the church upon my father's arm. I was conscious only of God above me, and Rupert waiting for me, and of the warm rays of sunlight which, as presently I knelt beside him, fell around us both.

Oh, what a fool I was—what an utter, utter fool!

From the hour of my marriage, I set myself to fulfil in myself and for his sake my highest dreams of womanhood. For Rupert's sake! Had he even guessed at it, how he must have laughed at me! That handsome, pleasure-loving boy, whose bests in life were good wine and good horses, good stories, good cigars, gaiety, ease, and light coquettish women! He wanted a wife to surprise, tease, and amuse him—I gave him a wife unfailingly true and tender. He wanted comic opera and I offered him an epic. He wanted something sparkling to while away the time with, and I offered him the unchangeable stars and the still, mystic moon.

He had fallen into the lure of an enchantress, and now the enchantress was gone. No wonder he grew bored. No wonder he was sick of the stars and the moon. He was only a handsome, pleasure-loving boy, and I—what was I? A woman who loved him as no one expects or desires to be loved to-day.

Dolores would have suited him completely. I knew that presently; and when I did know it, I killed the two of them.

I am writing confusedly. I must not grow confused. I must keep events clearly in my mind, for I have not much time.

But I must try to make you understand. You are so different—so cold, so hard. Perhaps, after all, it is useless. Perhaps, like all the others, you will only continue to hate and fear. As Rupert did, as my father did, as little, little Helga did. She was so like that other baby, your baby that I killed. Oh, my God, how many I have killed!

I must keep clear. I must not grow confused. I have only a few hours left.

Three years passed. Little Helga was two years old. The prettiest age! Like your baby's, her hair was fine gold, and fell in ringlets. I always twined them myself.

We were ordered to Ireland. I was glad. Rupert had been more than usually restless and bored. Army life in peace-time is too idle—all amusement and flirting and drinking. Rupert, I knew, was drinking far more than was good for him, and gambling heavily too. Large as our income was, we were always in debt. We entertained a great deal. I did not care for all these people. I had begun to hate the Army women, with their intriguing and wire-pulling and promotion-wangling. And the men seemed to expect me to flirt with them as they saw their own wives doing with other women's husbands. Fools! Had they ever loved anyone, I wondered, so that the rest of the world went out like a candle in the sunshine? But such a question, regarding such people, was merely an absurdity.

Still, Rupert liked them, and so I filled the house with them. I did not care for the perpetual dancing and hunting and luncheons and dinners. They kept me from little Helga. But Rupert did. So I made of our life together a ceaseless round of gaiety. Our life together? We were scarcely ever alone together. Whenever we were, Rupert became bored.

But he was proud of me. I was a good hostess. And whenever he was worried about things, he came to me. Perhaps, after all, in his own way he cared for me... No... he could not have... for when *she* came...

When I set foot on the shores of Ireland I knew that here my tragedy awaited me. The great, mournful hills; the wild, screaming birds; the intensely green land set amid the blue stormy waters: all filled me with a misery and foreboding that I scarcely knew how to conceal.

That land is set for tragedy. Has not its history been one long tragedy? Yet I think, too, that there, as in my mother's country, one might find some that worshipped the old ideals, the old gods...

The Dolores whom I met again in Ireland was another Dolores from the girl who had been my bridesmaid.

This Dolores was older, and something in her had strengthened and developed in an inexplicable way. Perhaps, long ago, I had made her suffer more than I knew.

She was thinner and paler and more languid. The pretty kitten had lengthened into a beautiful cat—sinuous, feline. Her dark eyes were shadowy and treacherous, her red mouth cynical. She had increased in subtlety, and had all the accomplished ways of a woman of the world.

Voltaire was dead, and he had left her rich. With him, I thought, had gone the last vestiges of girlhood that Dolores had ever had. She had always been mature and worldly-wise. Now she had the manners of a woman steeped in intrigue.

But apparently she was fascinating. Rupert found her so. Soon I began to learn what those things are for which the men of our day love women best.

"You have changed," she said to me that first day, sitting in our long, cool drawing-room.

In some frightful way I felt that history was repeating itself. She was regarding me in the half-amused, half-curious fashion she had often done in girlhood. Did she know that I was powerless now to harm her? And Rupert was laughing as he had done that night long ago, when I had worn a golden gown and suddenly awakened from a golden dream.

History repeats itself.

As before, we danced and rode and talked and played the days and nights away. Beneath all I did something whispered in me, "It will happen all over again."

She was there all the time. They were always together. She was witty and daring, wicked and sophisticated. She hated me. Presently she was able to make me repay a thousandfold for all I had made her suffer.

Rupert became restless and miserable. I knew he was drinking heavily. I knew he was ashamed of himself, that he avoided me, avoided little Helga. Dolores hated children. They bored her. Many things bored Dolores. Many things bored Rupert. But they did not bore each other.

History repeats itself.

And as the days went by, my soul within me trembled with fear. For I knew what I was going to do.

III

I t was the night of the —— Ball. I did not slip into the nursery as I always did before I went anywhere in the evening. I had gone in as usual to watch Nurse bathing Helga at half-past five that afternoon, and she had turned from me and clung to Maggie, screaming in terror.

It made me decide that I would not see her late in the day... Little children are very sensitive...

It was a very brilliant ball, and Dolores looked radiant and vivacious... Rupert, as the evening wore on, became moody and excited in turns. He was flushed, and far from sober. But, for all his muddlement, I caught him continually staring in a bewildered way at me.

Most people stared at me that night. I looked very wonderful... like a transparent flower lit up from within by a fire... Rupert wanted to dance with me, but I laughed him away, reminding him that men do not dance with their own wives.

As the night wore on, a change came over Dolores. She, too, looked at me covertly and often. In her face there was less bewilderment than fear. I believe she knew. All her sang-froid and worldly-wisdom gone, she stealthily watched me.

We went home rather early. Dolores could not avoid accompanying us. She was spending the night with us.

We three drove home through the darkness.

The road was rough. The night was wild. It was fine and clear, but high up in the sky the moon rode in and out of great black clouds, and the wind wailed and shrilled of coming storm.

Wild lights flared up every few moments on the hills... It was the gorse burning.

The leaping fires showed me Dolores' face, pale and frightened. It showed me Rupert's, drunkenly asleep. I laughed out loud in the darkness. The brougham stopped with a jerk.

Maloney came round to the window. I liked Maloney. A simple soul, but very fond of the bottle.

"Did ye hear that, ma'am?" he asked me. He was white, and smelling of whiskey.

"What?" I said.

"That sort of a laugh—like—like—"

"It was me, you fool," I said.

He looked at me.

"We'd best be not goin' on," he said.

I looked at him... He crossed himself and got back on the box... He whipped up the horses, and the carriage leapt forward.

On, on. Shaking and swaying and rattling. With that superstitious fool on the box, lashing the horses and crossing himself and muttering Hail Marys. With Dolores, her hands tight clasped upon her knees. With Rupert, snoring like the swine whom Circe has enchanted. And I, laughing every now and then into the darkness, because of the wildness in the sky, the wildness in the hills, the wildness in my soul.

A bright fire was burning in my room and my maid was there waiting for me. I sent her away and sat down to wait.

After a while I got up and went to my medicine-chest and took something out of it. Then I left my room and went to that of Dolores.

She opened her door unwillingly. She was ready for bed, her dark hair round her face, looking quite young in her long nightgown. Her eyes were big and dark and afraid.

I went past her and sat down by her fire. She closed the door reluctantly and followed me.

"Sit down," I said.

She did so. She sat there looking at me; then she began to cry.

Such weak, childish crying. And then she began to plead for mercy.

"Don't, don't, Helga," she kept saying. "Don't—don't—"

I held out something to her. A little bottle. "You often take these? To make you sleep?"

She shivered.

"You do?"

She nodded weakly.

"So no one would be surprised at your taking them to-night?"

She shook her head.

"How many do you take generally?"

Her voice was scarcely above a whisper as she muttered:

"Never more than two."

I put the bottle into her hand. She tried not to take it, but I kept my eyes on her, and her fingers closed round it.

"You will take six—now."

She sat there, moaning.

"You will take six—now."

She got up, went across the room, poured out water.

"Now," I said, my eyes on hers.

"One. Two. Three. Four. Five. Six."

I counted.

I got up. I went to her. "When I leave the room," I said, "you will lock yourself in and get into bed and put out the light."

Her eyes, large, agonised, were fixed on me.

"Sleep well," I said. "And dream—of Rupert."

Outside her room I waited.

The key turned in the lock. The bed creaked. The chink of light under the door went black.

"Good night, Dolores."

I returned to my room. I made up a great fire; and sat up beside it, laughing and laughing, until the dawn came.

At seven o'clock Nurse came to tell me that little Helga was very ill.

IV

Doctor McGrath did not come till lunch-time. He had been out at a country case, and the message had been delivered on his return.

I heard his ring, but he did not come up to me. I supposed the hall to be full of servants, pouring into his ears, in Irish fashion, their incredible tale.

The lovely young crathur, God rest her soul—and a Protestant an' all—dead in her bed, God save us all—an' the saints be betwane us an' harm—an' no raison sure at all at all—an' the misthress settin' up in the nursery an' not carin' more than if someone had just told her the fire was smokin'—an' the master, God save him, slapin' off the whiskey that was in him—

Fough!... I rang the bell sharply and repeatedly until the white-faced girl answered it.

"Send the doctor up here," I said.

"Sure, ma'am, he is lookin' at the corpse," she said.

"He can do that presently," I answered her. "My child is ill."

She went quickly.

Soon he came in, looking terribly agitated. "This is a frightful business," he said to me.

"You can do nothing for Mrs Dickinson," I said. "The baby has been like this since six. Why were you not here before?"

Abashed by my tone, he went over to the cot. The little thing lay there, deeply flushed and apparently asleep, yet her eyes were slightly open. He felt her pulse, took out his stethoscope, his face intensely grave.

"When did this start?" he asked me.

"I don't know. She was all right yesterday."

"Any severe shock—fright—any sign of convulsions?"

Shock? Fright? I remembered.

"She was unlike herself—nervous—screaming, yesterday in her bath," I told him.

"I will send in a nurse at once," he said. "Remain with her yourself till she comes..." He gave me a few directions... and left me—to go back to the dead Dolores.

I sat there hour after hour... I heard bells ring, vehicles come and go from the hall door. What were they? Police? Coroner? I did not greatly care... I knew that my child was going to die.

A nurse came in presently, and busied herself about the cot, and put useless paraphernalia about the room. Doctor McGrath came several times. He conferred with the nurse in low tones. They looked at me, where I still sat, huddled by the fire. I heard them talking about me.

"Terrible for her... the awful shock... and now this... Her husband should be with her... Get the maids to make her eat something..."

He approached me.

"Mrs Stourcross,... will you come to your room and lie down for a little? Believe me, there is nothing here that you can do."

"There is nothing here that anyone can do," I said.

"Nonsense," he said, meaning to be kind. "We shall pull her through. You have the best nurse in Dublin. Trust us, Mrs Stourcross, to do everything humanly possible."

I answered dully: "This is not humanly possible. This is God's punishment. I have killed her. She will die."

"Nonsense, nonsense," he exclaimed hurriedly. "You are unhinged. No wonder. It is a frightful business altogether... Where is your husband?"

"Still drunk, I expect," I told him, and he turned away.

"Let me sit here," I said to them. "I shall do her no harm now. And if she wakes, she may perhaps know me, and kiss me good-bye."

They pestered me no more. They brought me food, which I did not touch. I sat on, watching the cot and listening to the rising gale, which had been steadily increasing all day. The wind was shrieking round the house. Rain fell in torrents and as suddenly ceased. In the pauses of the wind came distant mutterings of thunder.

After a long time the dusk fell.

And as I leaned forward in my chair, all my soul concentrated on the face of my sleeping baby. I became conscious that the darkness was growing very rapidly in the room. It gathered till I could see nothing. Scarcely breathing, I fought it with every power that I possessed, for I knew what it meant. I could not force it back...

And then I heard the waters running clearly... And the multitude of feet upon their mournful way... and the high heartbreaking voices upon the swirling of the wind... and words...

When I opened my eyes the nurse was leaning over me. She was whispering to me.

"You were asleep," she said, "but I came over to tell you that your darling is waking. Come close, very quietly. When she wakes she will see you first and not a stranger."

"No, no," I said. "I must go away. I must go away."

There was very little light in the room and that only from a lamp behind a screen. As I got upon my feet, I could see the little form in the cot, the crumpled hand flung out upon the coverlet, the tangle of gold I had so often kissed... the shut eyes...

Slowly they opened... and fixed themselves on me.

Oh, God, when I am dead, let me then forget the look—the look—that came into those eyes...

I ran from her to the door... I could see her little hands beating feebly at the air... beating something away—

I opened the door and ran out into the corridor... But it followed me... the awful sound... in the silent house... of little Helga's frenzied screaming...

At the foot of the stairs I saw Rupert. He was standing there, his face lifted and ashen, listening.

"What is it?" he muttered. "My God—that isn't the child—it can't be the child?"

"Do you hear it?" I asked him. "Have you ever heard a child scream like that before? It is *your* child, screaming her life away."

I hated him more at that moment than I had ever loved him. I hated his weak, beautiful mouth that I had so often kissed; his dark, thick hair that I had so often caressed. I hated his white, coward's face—his staring, bewildered eyes; the fear of me that looked at me out of them.

"Go and get drunk again," I mocked him. "Dolores is dead—I killed her. Your child is dying—I killed her... Do you know what you are?... And what I am? For your sake?"

He stood there looking at me in the same paralysed way as Dolores had done. I do not know whether he even heard me... But I know he *saw*...

"You are the man I love," I said. "And have rejected God for. You are the man I now walk in Hell for, in such anguish as such as you cannot even conceive. You are a weak, charming thing, not worth anyone's love. But I love you—I love you... Haven't I finished with my child for you—my God for you? Can't you understand? Can't

you see? I cannot bear what I am going through. I cannot bear it...
Help me, Rupert... help me—"

He help me! He backed against the wall. *He* go down with me
into the dark places and wrestle with That Horror which I now could
no longer keep away! He stared at me like the craven fool he was.

"Get out the new mare," I said then to him, mocking and low,
"and ride her. Ride her till you break her neck and yours..."

A blinding flash of lightning lit up the staircase. The windows
rattled as if a devil was tearing at them. The storm had broken.

And I heard the voices singing, high and sweet and terribly sad...
I heard the feet of that sorrowful multitude upon their journey... And
I knew that they were the feet of all those through all the ages who
go down to Hell for love of human love.

And I knew that, for a little space at least, great power was given
to me. Not power to bless or heal or save, but power to rend, to
kill, to destroy.

"Go out and ride," I called to him. "Ride out into this storm, and
break her neck and yours."

He turned and went.

And in the morning they brought him to me, upon a stretcher, feet
first, and his face covered.

And in the morning they came to me and told me that my child
was dead.

V

I have heard people—comfortable people with foolish faces—explain why no one can any longer believe in such a place as Hell.

I could have told them things which would have driven the silly smile from their faces for ever had they believed them. But they would have said that I was mad.

"Seeking peace, and finding none." That is what you should write above my grave. Only it was not peace I sought through all those years. What have such as I to do with peace? Not peace—but a way back to Rupert and little Helga.

That was all I wanted. How gladly I would have died at any moment had I thought that death would have taken me any nearer to them. But I knew that the Thing which was with me would never let me come near to them.

Would not I and It, despairingly following after her, set little Helga screaming far away in Paradise?

I shuddered, and lived on. Death was more terrible than life, unless—until I found the way back.

But I never found the way back.

I was consumed, all those years, by a fire of hatred towards God and man.

I loathed my fellow-creatures. It seemed to me that their happiness mocked my misery.

How much simple happiness there is in the world! We only

realise how much there is for everyone when we ourselves are shut out from it by some devouring grief.

I did terrible things in those years. Everywhere I went I believe I brought unhappiness and wickedness and fear. I believe that everyone I met instinctively hated me. John did, until I hypnotised him. You did, until I hypnotised you.

I used to sit alone by the hour in my little room (I wandered from hotel to hotel, never staying longer than a few weeks in any place), concentratedly thinking hatred to certain people, consciously wishing evil—specified evil—to happen to them. I singled out those who struck me as being particularly happy and free from care.

And I made things happen. Terrible things. Cruel things. Then I would laugh at the God I defied and tell Him that I, too, could send out punishments. I, too, could kill things, maim things, which had offended me. It was an offence to me that that light-hearted Italian woman should have a little laughing child to love... My child was dead. God and I had killed it... The Shadow and I together, brooding, brooding, would cripple her child. We did. We had great power... It and I.

But I could not find the way back.

I was in Egypt, far away from anyone I had ever known, when, six months after your father's death, you were born.

When I knew you were coming to me, I was filled with horror. What manner of child could this be? That God, whom some miscalled a God of Love, but who was really a God of Hatred, was going to heap yet more punishment upon me. How I hated you, unborn and undesired! I had one child, and He and I had killed her; and though I might search the world for a path to lead me to her again, that same God would hide the way from me. What hideous mockery lay hidden in the coming of this second child?

When you came you were as lovely as a dream. I lay and looked at you. I remembered. There had been a time—long ago, before *she* came back, before I had gone into the shadows to seek this horrible Thing again—there had been a time when my whole life had been set towards loveliness. Out of those futile dreamings, out of my love for Rupert, you had come.

I sent you away to a foster-mother. I could not bear to look at you. You hurt too much... you hurt too much... I would not have you near me.

As soon as it was possible you were taken home to my father.

Fourteen years went by. I never found the way back to Rupert and little Helga.

I began to realise something. The soul that has turned from good and chosen evil can never find its own way back. It is in darkness, blinded.

But if one, loving and sinless, so will, that one can bring light to its darkness.

This is a marvellous truth. I, from my place in Hell, tell you that this is the basic truth at the heart of Christianity. This is the real mystery behind all religions. But few, of whatever religion, realise its true significance.

In this world there are many souls in darkness. In this world there are some souls loving and sinless... Whenever, wherever these two meet and touch each other, the light breaks.

At that contact (always *contact*) the blind eyes see, the deaf ears hear. The soul knows its way back. That way back may be very terrible. It may lead down to death, down to Hell... But the soul that was blind has seen it. One day, sooner or later, it cannot choose but go.

When I knew this, I went to find you.

For my father wrote to me that you had the nature of an angel.

I would go to you, make you love me, make you pity me; and you would show me the way back.

But you, too, feared and hated me.

As everything else did, you shrank from me. When I told you I was going to take you to live with me, you looked ready to cry.

You clung to my father. He, poor man, had grown to love you in his old age as he had never found time to love me. He was growing feeble. You were sunshine and youth in his house, sunshine and youth and love. You clung to him, but he no less clung to you.

The old storm rose in me. Was *nothing* that I possessed to love me? Something must love me; I knew that now. You were my own child. You should; you must; I would make you.

Hatred of my father surged up, too. Was he to come first with you, when you belonged to me?

In a few days he died. He was old, he was feeble, and I sat before my fire upstairs for three whole nights without sleeping, as I had acquired the habit of doing... Brooding, brooding, It and I... On the fourth day he died.

The last afternoon I was sitting beside him... He was very weak; the doctor thought that before evening the end would come. I fixed my eyes on his, willing that he should open them.

In a few hours at most he would have passed away. Now that he was so near to death, so likely to understand, I wanted to tell him my terrible need and despair. I wanted to tell him why I must have you...

Slowly the heavy lids raised themselves. He looked at me, first unseeingly. Then his look changed to recognition and a sort of piteous distress.

He tried to lift his weak hands, warding me away. His lips moved, his eyes filmed over. His head fell back. He was dead.

Dead. With a look on his face of utter horror and repugnance.

He was the only good man I ever met. And fear and hatred were all that he could feel for me... The loving *and* sinless must be very, very few.

I took you away with me. You came because you could do nothing else... came, in like fear and hatred, your eyes large and your lips trembling...

Like all young, happy, healthy things, you would have none of me.

Living with me, you ceased to be either healthy or happy. You moped about, became ill. The doctor to whom I went told me to send you to school.

I did so. In the holidays you came back to me, shrinking certainly, but well and normal. I began to hypnotise you.

When I ordered you to love me, you followed me about like a little wistful dog, waiting on me, fetching and carrying for me. But such love as that could never help me.

When I let you out of my power you were nervous, shaken, and resentful. Often I found your large eyes on me, filled with that mingling of dislike and fear.

Sometimes That which was with me made me very cruel to you. Angry and baffled because you were out of my reach, I took savage delight in showing you some of my power... Since you would not love me, I would make you know you had good cause to fear me. I did make you know it.

You remember that little boy you played with? You told Doctor Toogood I had killed him. It was true. Deliberately, concentratedly, to frighten you, I willed that he should die.

You remember your dog? I killed that also. But dogs are funny creatures, easily destroyed by psychic force. I killed one before— Zinera's dog—by accident.

There was, too, that good-natured, fat, foolish landlady that you were so fond of...

You used to wonder how I did it. You came to realise after a little that I had to have certain circumstances in which to do it. I had to have personal contact with the things I destroyed. And I myself had to be in a special state of mind.

In short, I had to be in contact with Something from which I drew the power; and also in contact with the thing I hated and wished to destroy.

You used to act upon this knowledge... When you thought I was concentrating upon a victim, you tried to prevent me from sending gifts or letters to that victim. I often laughed to see your futile manœuvring.

You grew up; and then John came. Quite spontaneously you loved John.

At first I was surprised. I had not thought you of the kind that is capable of love. Then I was glad... Many things would now become clear to you... When you had learnt the love that fire cannot quench nor waters drown, out of the fullness of your heart you would love and pity even me.

I let you love and marry John.

For a long time you would not marry him. I knew why, and all the fear you had. I set myself to still that fear.

I hypnotised John. He began to like me. I was unfailingly charming to him. I saw bewilderment in your face, then joy.

I let you marry John.

And when you were married, and went away from me, I saw all the gladness in your face as you left me... And I knew that your love had taught you nothing.

You stood at the gate of a new world, a world amazingly sweet and clean and golden. You were leaving the old fears and glooms behind you. Almost with a visible shiver of relief, you were leaving *me* behind you. You stood alone together in God's sunlight—you and John.

Two fools in Paradise.

And I, alone, in Hell.

VI

If you would not save me, then for me there was no way back.

If you would not save me, I should never find Rupert or little Helga any more.

If you would not save me, I would take and destroy you and your John, as I had those others—those many, many others.

I do not know how many times I have nearly killed your John, and yet something has prevented it.

That breastplate I sent to France—he could never have worn it.

I took you away from him, and let him see just what you were in my hands—a creature without wish or will except to do what I told you.

But it did not make him turn from you. He followed, he and that man Toogood, and won you back again.

When Toogood fell down those steps, in my presence, why did he not kill himself? You must have had something to do with it. There must have been love in that house. Love—the love that is of God—has always defeated me.

It is stronger than hate, stronger than evil. You could love those strangers—John, that fat landlady long ago, that doctor, Toogood—why could you never love me? Why could you not love me and heal me?

No one has ever loved me...

When first I found you again, in your little cottage across the road, love was there also. Do you know how many times I have watched your cottage from my window? Watched you bring the baby in from the garden and get it ready for bed, kiss it and talk to it? Watched your lights go out, imploring you with all my heart to let some of that love shine out upon me?

"Lighten our darkness, O Love." That is the wordless prayer of all the souls that are in darkness.

I sent you letters—presents. One day I saw you burning them. I laughed aloud. Fool! Consumed by fear!

Fear! How afraid you were, the two of you! I knew then that there was no hope for me. For me there was no way back. I should never see Rupert or little Helga any more.

John came, in hate and fear, to beg me to go away. I laughed at him.

The glory went from your little home. The shadows of your own terrors, your own hatreds, filled it instead.

One day you, passing my window, sent that loathing, frightened glance at me. The power that was with me struck you and you fell down senseless.

Darkness dwelt in your house. And in mine?... I am always in darkness.

That last evening, when John was out, I went into your cottage. I wanted to see you—to see the place where Love had been, and which I had made desolate. The nurse was a fool. It was quite easy.

Not a trace of happiness remained in it. I was thinking that when, across the landing, I heard a little cooing. It was the baby.

I crossed over and pushed the slightly open door. It was there in its cot, playing softly with its toes. Its little face was beaming with satisfaction at its own cleverness. It pulled up one toe after another, gurgling with pleasure.

A lovely little thing. Fair, fragile, golden—and terribly, cruelly like little Helga.

I watched it. It was so engrossed that it did not see me. But presently it would look up and see me.

Something rose in my throat. I waited, scarcely breathing. What would its eyes be like when at last it did see me? Some tremendous issue seemed to hang upon that glance—some issue, involving—

It looked up. Saw me. Stopped playing with its toes. Its face changed, became frightened, troubled. I came nearer. Spoke to it. Bent over it. Held out my arms to it, wordlessly pleading—pleading...

It smiled softly, wistfully. A strange smile for so young a child. Troubled, pitiful. As if it felt sorry for the strange thing it saw. Perhaps the sorrow of that little angel soul outweighed its fear.

I bent and lifted it. It twined its arms round my neck, sweetly putting its face to mine. I kissed it again and again.

A long time after, I put it back into its cot and went away. At the door I turned back for one more look at it. It was lying as I had put it, gold head upon white pillow, looking after me with that same wistful, troubled, loving little smile.

I went out of the house. I did not want to see you again. I did not want to meet John, or gloat over him... I had seen something. There was something that I must do—do quickly... Presently, if I sat down and thought about it, I should realise what it was.

Next evening they told me the little thing was dead.

They buried it to-day. I know what it is that I have to do. I have to go away and take the dark Thing with me, and leave the world clean for you and John and the children that will come to you. I have to do it now, before I and It can do any more harm.

We have to go away; away from you, from Rupert, from little Helga, from your dead baby. Away from hope, away from love. Away from everything we can do harm to.

I began to write this in the early dawn, as soon as I knew what it was that I must do. When I began it, I did not see things as clearly as I do now. I see things very clearly now.

I see what I am, what I have done. I see that It must go away. And since I cannot send It away, I must go with It. So that we can never do any more harm.

I have finished—finished paper, candles, everything. Everything but that stuff in the glass. It takes time to work, they say—I will take it now. Nothing to do then, but make a parcel of this for you to read—not now, but presently, when you hate me less.

It is quite dark—not even a star. Only the light in your window.

That has gone out, too.

The night is as still as Death.

It is nasty-smelling stuff.

I hear footsteps in the road. That fool of a nurse again. No—a man. He is at the gate, coming up the path. I must be quick. No one shall stop me now.

I have finished it.

And it tasted—sweet.

ACKNOWLEDGEMENTS

Researching authors lost to time is an intricate, often frustrating puzzle to solve, so I'd like to thank everyone behind the scenes who at least stopped me going absolutely insane for a spell while I tried to piece together the story of the Corse-Scotts' life. Thanks go to Caroline Jones of Wellington College for early insights into Edward and Ernle Corse-Scott, Daisy at Castleman Estate Agents in Verwood, Melanie at St Michael's Church in Verwood, June at Verwood Heathland Heritage Centre, Phillip Corse-Scott from Takanini, who had no idea about who his distant relatives were until I told him(!), Mike Ashley, and Sue Smith from St Heliers Bowling Club who finally helped me reach a direct relative of Rosalie and Edward. Special mention must go to Rosalie and Edward's grandson, John Herring (Corse-Scott) from Auckland, for his incredible help, photos of Rosalie and Edward and additional information on his relatives, and last but not least, Jonny Davidson, who has been on this journey with me from the start and came up with some good, early information on Rosalie and Edward.

JM

ALSO AVAILABLE

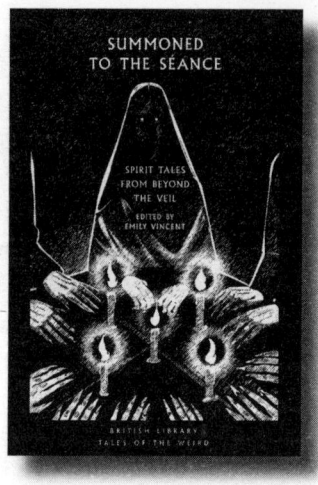

You will hear loud raps, you will have your faces touched by cold, damp, unseen fingers—THINGS will be all round you, and a frightful white face will come out of nowhere, and peer into yours!

Through the electric silence of the séance, a terrible, hurtling force draws near. A play with the planchette invites a diabolical visitor to Radley Manor. A medium's summoning of a lost child pitches them into mortal peril.

In this haunting new collection, Emily Vincent presents fourteen chilling classics and lost gems of séance fiction which evoke the most thrilling and thought-provoking aspects of the popular Victorian movement of spiritualism.

Featuring tales by practising mediums, sceptics and ghost-seekers including Arthur Conan Doyle, H. G. Wells, Florence Marryat and F. Scott Fitzgerald, this volume is a suffusion of spectral frights and satirical skewerings, destined to linger with the reader long after the door to the séance has closed.

ALSO AVAILABLE

"The Sound builds; sound destroys; and invisible sound-vibrations affect concrete matter. For all sounds produce forms—the forms that correspond to them, as you shall now see..."

When Robert Spinrobin answers an advert seeking a tenor singer with a grasp of ancient languages, he soon finds himself summoned to the Welsh mountain home of the ex-clergyman Philip Skale. Here Skale, the housekeeper Mrs. Mawle and her niece, Miriam, have been pursuing a new science, using sound and song to intone the true names of people and matter—and recording the uncanny phenomena conjured through this naming ritual.

But there is a question humming at the heart of Skale's plans: what if the quartet could use harmony to harness a forbidden name beyond the preserve of humanity? As the singers gain momentum, a gathering storm of disastrous cosmic consequences glowers on the horizon in this original and fast-paced novel, first published in 1910.

For more Tales of the Weird titles
visit the British Library Shop (shop.bl.uk)

We welcome any suggestions, corrections or feedback you may have, and will
aim to respond to all items addressed to the following:

The Editor (Tales of the Weird), British Library Publishing,
The British Library, 96 Euston Road, London NWI 2DB

We also welcome enquiries through our social media accounts, @BL_Publishing.